# Julie's Meadow

Tony Dwelly

Published by Tony Dwelly
Publishing partner: Paragon Publishing, Rothersthorpe
First published 2011
© Tony Dwelly 2011

The rights of Tony Dwelly to be identified as the author of this work have been asserted by him in accordance with the Copyright, Designs and Patents Act of 1988.

All rights reserved; no part of this publication may be reproduced, stored in a retrieval system, or transmitted in any form or by any means, electronic, mechanical, photocopying, recording or otherwise without the prior written consent of the publisher or a licence permitting copying in the UK issued by the Copyright Licensing Agency Ltd, www.cla.co.uk

ISBN 978-1-907611-91-9

Book design, layout and production management by Into Print
www.intoprint.net
01604 832149

Printed and bound in UK and USA by Lightning Source

# Chapter 1

It all started when Fred passed his driving test, June 1961.

Fred had a great pal named Julie. They lived next door to each other and had been inseparable all their lives. She was nineteen and engaged to be married in September to a local lad, Robert.

Although Robert worked hard, he spent more time shooting and fishing with his friend Julian Sleep than he ever did with Julie; if they weren't out fishing and shooting, they were down at the pub. It was as if Fred and Julie did all the things Robert and Julie should be doing.

On the day that Fred passed his test, he went in to Julie's house to give her the news. "That's good," she said, as she kissed him on the cheek.

"What are you doing Saturday?" she asked.

"Don't know yet. It depends on old grumpy farmer Higgins. I might have to work, as I've had half a day to take my test. Why, what did you want?" he asked.

"Do you remember Sarah Page and John Brite at school?"

"Yes," Fred replied, "you and Sarah were great friends, and they got married, a secret one I believe."

"That's right. Sarah's pregnant, but the biggest surprise is that Lord Trelivan has given them the tenancy of Tremarrow Farm as a wedding present, much to his son's disgust.

"Anyhow, I just wondered if you would drive me over to see them."

"We could go over on Sunday, if that's ok," Fred replied.

"I better just see what Robert has to say first," Julie replied.

"What do you see in him?"

"Shhh," she said, as she put her finger over his lips.

That evening, as Fred was going towards his car to take it out for a spin, Robert and Julie appeared around the corner.

"You're going to take Julie out to see her friend on Sunday?" Robert shouted. "Pretty safe with you, in't she. You wouldn't know a good pussy if you saw one." Julie went red with embarrassment and Fred just got in his car and drove off.

Sunday soon came around and Julie and Fred made their way to Tremarrow Farm, where they were met by Sarah's brother, George.

George was twenty-three and was autistic; I don't think back then there was a great understanding of this. George was a great character, and his love of animals was second to none.

Although George couldn't pronounce words, he understood what you said and had a canny way of making you understand him. It wasn't long before he had Fred and Julie over in the barn looking at his pet fox.

Sarah soon appeared. "Come on, George. Leave our guests alone," she said. George just smiled with his boyish smile. He had the kind of face that when he smiled you felt you just wanted to hug him.

"Let's go indoors," said Sarah, "We have lots to talk about. John will be back soon."

"You two go on," said Fred, "I'll stay and George can show me around." You could see George was happy with that.

George took Fred over to the field that joined onto the yard. As soon as George got to the gate a large, fat, black and white pig came running over to meet him.

With that, John drove into the yard. "Hi, Fred. Been a long time," he said as he stretched his hand out and shook hands firmly. "Come on. I'm gasping for a cuppa. What about you, George?" he said with a smile. George smiled with his boyish grin and they both followed John across the yard and into the kitchen.

The kitchen had a long pine table running down the

middle with three chairs on each side and two semicircular chairs, one at each end. There was an Aga cooker quite close to the table, which was lit, as it had Sunday roast cooking, omitting a smell that will remain with you always.

Sarah sat on the rounded chair at the top end of the table and Julie sat on one of the chairs at the side. You could see they were both glad to see each other and were engrossed in conversation.

"Any chance of a cuppa?" shouted John.

"You know where the kettle is," replied Sarah. "We've got too much catching up to do."

"I'll do it," said Julie, "if that's all right."

As Julie got up to get the kettle, she jumped, startled, as someone stood in the door way. It was Lord Trelivan's son, Rupert. "What do you want?" Sarah snapped.

"Charming," came the reply, "I'm just paying a visit on my tenants."

Sarah replied, "We're not your tenants."

"Not yet, darling, but one day soon," said Rupert, as he gave a little wave and turned and started to walk away. He suddenly turned back and said, "By the way, if I see that vermin your spastic brother's got in the barn, I'll give it both barrels," as he raised the twelve bore shotgun he had under his arm.

"You bastard," shouted Sarah.

"That's good, coming from you," Rupert replied. "I know who my father is. More than you and your stupid brother can say."

Sarah jumped up and started to make her way to the door. "Leave it," said John as he grabbed her gently by the arm and pulled her back.

A deadly silence filled the room; it seemed like ages passed.

Julie, still standing by the kettle, broke the silence. "Come on, how about this cuppa," she said as she walked over to the tap and filled the kettle.

"I'm so sorry, whatever must you think," said Sarah.

Fred replied, "I don't think you've got anything to be sorry for. In fact, I think you were quite calm under the circumstance."

"Let's not spoil the day," John said, as he turned to Fred. "Do you want to come up to the top meadow with me and have a look at the sheep, and the two girls can have a natter and get the dinner?"

"That'll do for me," Fred replied.

"Us, too," came the reply from the other end of the kitchen. The girls laughed when they realised they had both replied in tandem.

John and Fred made their way across the yard and through the gate into the lane.

Looking back, he could see George looking sad by the lane gate. John beckoned to him. "Come on," he shouted. He turned to Fred, "You don't mind, do you?"

"Not at all," was the reply.

As they walked up the lane, John started to explain to Fred. "We are very lucky," he said, "but in a difficult situation. Lord Trelivan gave us this tenancy when we got married, along with a hundred ewes and thirty suckle cows and their calves. And there's one hundred and sixty acres of wheat and barley. He also gave us a small sum of money to tie us over. All sounds too good to be true, doesn't it?"

"So far," replied Fred. "So what's the catch?"

"None as such; more of a thorn in the side." John went on to say, "Rupert Trelivan, he never has liked Sarah, and with Lord Trelivan being quite ill, he could soon inherit, and I am sure he would kick us out."

"Can he legally do that?" asked Fred.

"Oh, yes, he could soon find some little thing we've done

wrong. The main problems I have are, do I keep the ewe lambs for breeding, and the same for the heifer calves, or do I send them all for slaughter?"

"Are you asking me the question?" Fred replied.

"I would value your opinion. If I remember rightly, you had a wise head at school."

"Wise head that's a turn up for the books, but as I see it, if you can continue on here, you will need more stock, and my boss always says its better the stock you know. And in any case, in calf heifers always make good money if you had to sell. It might be a bit of hit and miss with lambs though."

"That makes sense. Who is that boss of yours?"

"Harold Higgins. Do you know him?" Fred replied.

"I've heard of him. Bit of an eccentric by all accord."

"He's a bit eccentric all right. Last week we were loading sheep. One jumped over the fence, so he shot it. He said, "I can't abide animals that won't do what they're supposed to." We had a pig that kept head-butting the bucket when you went to feed them. He picked it up and carried it up to the next farm and swapped it with one of theirs. When he got back, I said I was surprised they would swap. I asked him what they said. "Nothing," he said. "We don't speak. Fell out years ago.""

They had now reached the top of the lane, and all three of them leaned on the gate and watched the lambs, some frolicking in the sun, some climbing on their mothers backs and some just lazily lying down.

"Pretty sight, don't you think?" John said.

Fred just looked and nodded, and George's face just lit up like the cat that got the cream.

"Everything looks fine here. Let's get back and see if there is any dinner. What do you say, George?" John asked.

George nodded in agreement.

As they made their way across the yard, the smell of roast

beef was coming to meet them. You could almost taste the roast in the smell. "It smells like they have done a bit more than just talk," said Fred.

"Let's hope it tastes as good as it smells," replied John.

As they entered the kitchen, Sarah shouted, "About time, now. Wash your hands, sit up and shut up," in a nice joking way.

There was total silence as they sat and ate. When they had finished, Fred said, "I think it's because it's cooked in an Aga that makes it so good."

Sarah replied, "Thanks for the complement."

"Ahh, no, I didn't mean …" Fred was spluttering.

"Come on, spit it out," Julie said.

Fred took a long pause and then replied, "You are a smashing cook, but I think all food tastes better cooked in an Aga."

"I forgive you," said Sarah, smiling. "Now, where are we going to have a cup of tea – inside or out?"

"We'll go out on the patio, it's a nice afternoon, if that's all right with everyone," John replied.

Julie said, "You three go on. Me and Sarah will quickly do the dishes, then we'll be there."

They were all sitting out on the patio. Sarah had been talking about her baby, which was soon due, Julie about her wedding, John how they are about to start harvest. George had gone to play with his pet fox.

Suddenly Rupert Trelivan reappeared, still brandishing a shotgun. "I've come a hunting," he shouted. You could tell he had been drinking.

"Why don't you just leave us alone?" asked Sarah.

"I'll leave you alone when you get out of my farm," he replied.

"Why us? The estate has eight thousand acres and twelve farms," Sarah replied.

"Where do you want me to start?" said Rupert. "The fact that your mother was a peasant and a slut who tried to turn my father against me."

"How dare you," said Sarah, getting agitated and upset. "My mother was no slut and your father was upset with the way you behaved and still is. He doesn't need anyone to tell him, he knows you are a cad."

"No slut, ha," said Rupert. "Do you know who your father is, or your stupid brother's? No, I don't think you do. It's no wonder he's daft. Your mother was so stupid she couldn't cross the road."

John jumped up. "How dare you!" he shouted. "You are completely out of order and I want you off this land now." John was now about a foot away from his face.

This caught Rupert by surprise. His whole tone of voice changed, and he turned and started to walk away. As he did, he said, "Keep your hair on, I can't help if the truth hurts."

Sarah shouted after him, "Your mother left you because she couldn't stand you!"

Rupert's mother just vanished on his thirteenth birthday some twenty-nine years ago. Sarah's mother was her maid. When she left, Lord Trelivan was devastated. No one could think of any reason why she'd want to leave. Well, there could have been one reason – Rupert. Sarah's mother had told how there were times when he would kick his mother, punch her. On one occasion he stabbed her with a pen knife. She hid all this from Rupert's father, but when she vanished, Sarah's mum thought it only right that she should tell him.

This led to friction between Lord Trelivan and Rupert, which still lasts to today. Sarah's mother became quite close to Lord Trelivan over the years and suffered loads of abuse from Rupert. Unfortunately, she died in a tragic accident twelve months ago. It's believed, because of the tyre marks, she was knocked down by one car, then run over by another.

Neither car stopped and they have never been found. It was the same day that the estate's wages were stolen. It's believed that whoever stole the money ran her down just outside the gates.

Things settled down on the farm. Rupert had left, and normal chat had resumed. "Where are you going to live when you get married?" Sarah asked Julie.

"Robert's got a herdsman's job up near Oakhampton, and there's a cottage with the job. I'm not really looking forward to it. I like it where I am, really. Still, I expect I'll get used to it. Robert has to go up there on Wednesday to start, so I won't see him then until we get married."

"Would you like to come and stay with us until then?" Sarah asked.

"Love to," she replied. "I'll come over next Saturday, if that's all right."

"Of course it is," Sarah replied. "We would love that. Wouldn't we, John."

John nodded in approval.

"What about you, Fred," John asked. "Any girl in your life?"

"No time for that old nonsense," he replied.

"There must be someone you fancy," said Sarah in teasing way.

"Let's just say there is someone I'm very fond of, and I'm afraid she's going to get hurt."

Julie just looked at Fred and went bright red.

"That's enough of that sort of talk; me and Fred want to talk farming," John said, trying to change the subject.

The afternoon soon passed. Sarah had told Julie how sweet she thought Fred was and how lucky she was to have such a good friend.

Julie agreed, and told her that she had had a great day and was really looking forward to next week.

John reached out and shook Fred by the hand in a vice-like grip. "I hope we will see you next week," he said.

Sarah leaned over and kissed him on the cheek. "I'll let the Aga do the cooking, if you promise you'll come," she said.

"You'll have job to keep me away with an offer like that," Fred replied. "If you got a two-man job, make sure you save it to next weekend," he shouted as they drove off.

"Thanks for a wonderful day," Julie said as they drove home. "You got on well with John, didn't you?" she continued.

"A great guy. I like Sarah as well. I think she's got a lot to put up with, with that monster Rupert Trelivan. One thing that was quite clear – the love they both have for Sarah's brother." The tone of Fred's voice had changed. You could tell he had a lump in his throat.

Sarah looked over at Fred; she could see a tear in his eye. "You are a dear," she said. They arrived home, and just before Julie went indoors, she put her arms around Fred and gave him a big hug, and as she broke away, she gently kissed him on the cheek.

Fred went in with a big smile on his face; she had never done that before.

The following Saturday, Fred shouted into Julie, "Got your case packed, Jew?"

"You're early," she shouted back, "it's only quarter to eight."

"Yes, well, John told me so much about Sarah's fried breakfasts, he said he would go out and see the stock, and if we get there about eight thirty, we will be just in time for breakfast."

"You and your food," she replied as she came out the door carrying her case.

"You're travelling light. I expected you to have a big

trunk," Fred said, smiling as if he had just cracked the joke of the year.

"Well, I thought if I haven't got something, you can always get it for me. Anyway, what's this Jew bit?" she asked. As they got in the car and drove off.

"That's my new name for you, my little jewel. Anyway, I haven't seen much of you this week, What have you been up to?"

"Oh, this and that," she replied. "I spent a couple days with Robert before he went, and I spent a bit of time with wedding arrangements. There's lots to do, you know."

"You're still going ahead with it, then," Fred said with a tone of dismay in his voice.

"Why shouldn't I?" she replied.

"I thought you might have seen some sense. Anyway, let's not talk about it. Let's just enjoy the weekend," Fred said as they pulled into John and Sarah's yard.

As they got out of the car, George came running over and grabbed Fred by the arm and guided him over to the gate in the corner of the yard. The large saddleback pig came running over with eleven baby piglets following behind. I don't know who had the biggest smile, George, the pig, or Fred.

"You pair coming for breakfast?" John shouted. Fred put his arm around George as they went over to the kitchen. "She was a clever girl, wasn't she," he said. If you could have bottled George's face that day, you could have sold it for a fortune.

They all went into the kitchen and sat down to a hearty, fried breakfast.

Julie was quite through breakfast. "You all right?" Sarah asked, "You look miles away. Thinking about Robert, I suppose."

Julie just looked up and smiled in reply. John turned to Fred. "Four of the red Devon cows are going to calf in the next couple of days," he said. "Will you give me a hand to move them? I want to bring them down to the back meadow. I just get a bit concerned where they are, as the old mill pond is there and it's not fenced off and its twelve foot deep in places. Last thing we want is a calf falling in there."

Up they got and made their way out the door. George just sat there. John knew he was waiting for him to ask him to come. John whispered to Fred, "You ask him."

They stopped in the door way. "What about George," Fred said, "Is he coming to help?" George's face just lit up as John said, "I don't expect we could do it without him," and off the three of them went.

Julie was doing the washing up. Sarah went over to her and put her arm around her. "Now, missus, sit down and tell me what's wrong."

"Nothing," she said, as she wiped a tear from her eye.

"You can't fool me, Julie. I know there's something," Sarah said sternly.

"If you must know, I think I'm in love," Julie blurted out.

Sarah quickly replied, "that's good, isn't it? You're supposed to be in love when you get married."

"That's the problem. It's not Robert. I think after all these years as great friends, I have just fallen in love with Fred."

"How do you know? You might just be feeling a bit anxious with the wedding coming up." You could tell by the tone in Sarah's voice she was trying to comfort her.

"No, it's different," Julie said as she sat back in the chair. "Last week I gave him a hug, and my stomach ached. It was a feeling that I've never felt before. We haven't seen each other all week, and I just couldn't wait to see him. When he called for me this morning, I had that same feeling."

"I'm lost for words. I always thought you and Fred would end up together when you were younger, but what about Robert?" Sarah asked.

"I just don't know. I don't love him. Never have. We were pushed together by our families; they were great friends and we saw a lot of each other. Robert has never asked me to marry him. It was our families that fixed the date and we just sort of went along with it." Julie was struggling to hold back the tears as she confided in Sarah. "Would you be surprised if told you we had never made love? In fact, Robert never so much as touched me and I don't want him to. There's just no feeling there."

Still flabbergasted, Sarah asked, "What are you going to do? Does Fred know how you feel?"

"No, and don't you dare mention it. If he doesn't feel the same way, it could spoil a great friendship, and I couldn't bear that," Julie replied.

"Oh, Julie, dear, can't you see that boy's deeply in love with you?" Sarah went on, "He only goes along with your relationship with Robert because he is sure that's what you want."

"I don't know. I don't want to risk saying anything at the moment. If something is meant to happen, it will." Little did Julie know how soon that might be.

The three men had just arrived back in the yard. George had shown Fred a baggers set down by the stream in the lower meadow. Fred was quite taken back by the meadow. There was a stream running through the middle and at the top end there was a deep pool.

John had explained that it was the old mill pond. The water was crystal clear and the meadow was full of wild flowers. John had said he wanted to keep it just as it was. "And who could blame him?" Fred thought. It was just beautiful.

"Put the kettle on," John shouted, as they got to the door of the house.

"What does anyone want for lunch?" Sarah asked.

"I couldn't eat another thing after that big breakfast your Aga cooked," Fred said jokingly.

"You're getting a little cheeky, Mr." Sarah replied. "What about the rest of you?"

"We're fine," was the reply.

Sarah glanced out of the window. Miss Pollard from up at the big house came riding into the yard on her bike. "Hi, Sarah," she shouted.

Sarah returned the greeting. "It's nice to see you. To what do we owe this visit?"

"It's Lord Trelivan. He's very ill. The doctor doesn't think he'll last the night, and he's asking to see you and George."

"I'll put your bike in the boot and we'll come right over," John said as he turned to Julie and Fred. "You pair don't mind, do you?"

"No, not at all," Fred replied.

"Just make yourselves at home and we'll be back as quick as we can," Sarah shouted as she struggled to get George into the car. Miss Pollard was sweating profusely. It was a very hot day and she had ridden her bike up a very steep hill.

"I don't suppose I could have a drink of water before we go?" she asked.

"I'll get it," Julie shouted. She ran into the kitchen and returned with a glass of water. Miss Pollard downed it in one and climbed into the car.

"That drink of water looked good," Fred commented to Julie. "All right, I can take a hint," she said and went off and returned with two glasses of water. They sat down on the bench outside the door. Fred told her all about the meadow and stream. He sounded quite excited.

Julie jumped up and held her hand out. "Show me," she said in an excited voice.

They walked up across the first field, hand in hand. I don't think Fred realised what he was doing. They reached the meadow and walked slowly through the flowers, until they reached the mill pond. It looked wonderful, with crystal clear water, and had a mirror image of a horse chestnut tree that stood on the far bank running down the middle.

They sat down beside the pond. It was really hot. "Can we go in?" Julie asked.

Fred looked startled. "What, with our clothes on?" he replied.

"No, silly. You turn your back and I'll get undressed and get in, then I'll turn around whilst you get in."

"If you say so," he said nervously. Fred turned to look up the field as Julie got undressed and got in the water. "God, it's cold," she said. "Quick, Fred, get undressed. I can't stand still long."

Fred started to get undressed. He looked at Julie's pile of clothes and saw her bra on top of the pile.

"Have you taken everything off?" he gasped.

"All except my knickers," she replied. "Now come on, or else I'll freeze to death."

Fred quickly got down to his y-fronts and jumped in. They splashed around for a couple of minutes, but it was far too cold.

"How we going to dry ourselves?" Fred asked. "We can't put wet clothes on."

"No worries," said Julie, "we'll just lie down in the sun until we dry."

"With no clothes on?" Fred replied, startled.

"Why not?" she replied. "You never used to worry when your mother babysat for my mum and she washed us both in the sink."

"Yeah, I was four then. I'm a bit bigger now."

"Just a bit?" she asked jokingly.

Fred got out of the water first.

As he stood on the bank and looked, he saw Julie standing with water up to her waist. Her breasts looked firm and round. "God," he thought, "she's beautiful." He had never noticed her in that way before. As she walked out of the water, Fred looked straight at her. He just blurted it out, "You're the most beautiful thing I have ever seen."

"I'll take that as a compliment, shall I?" she replied, with a big smile on her face. They lay down on the grass facing each other; her face was only inches away from his.

"Fred, I have something to tell you," she said softly. "I do want to get married."

Fred started to turn around. "Don't spoil the day," he said. She put one arm around him and pulled him back with her other hand. She put a finger over his lips. "Shhh, let me finish," she said, as she pulled him close to her. "I do want to get married one day, but not to Robert."

"I don't understand. What do you mean?" Fred was confused.

"What I'm saying is that I'm not going to marry Robert. I don't love him and I never have."

Fred jumped up, picked their clothes up and threw them up in the air. "That's wonderful," he shouted. He fell back on the ground and rolled over towards her. Their eyes sparkled as their lips met. They kissed passionately. His hands explored the whole of her body as they made love.

It was as if it had been bottled up inside them for years, and today was the day the cork blew out. After they had made love, they just lay all afternoon in each other's arms.

The next thing they heard was John shouting from a distance.

"Quick, get dressed," Julie said, with a mixture of fear and excitement. They soon got their clothes on and ran down the meadow.

As they came through the gate, they jumped several feet as a voice from the other side said, "Ah, there you are." It was John. "I thought I'd go in to Tavistock and get Chinese, if that's all right with you pair."

"That's fine with me," they replied in tandem. "I'll come with you," Fred said, hoping he was acting normal.

"How was the sick?" Fred enquired, as they made their way to Tavistock.

"Not very good. Sarah's quite upset. They don't think he'll last the night." John had tears in his eyes, and he found it hard to continue. But he managed to say how Lord Trelivan had told them not to worry about the farm.

He knew what was going on with Rupert. He said, "He's been a problem all his life. He has robbed, bullied, and broke our hearts, but I've just been too weak to deal with it." Then just as they were about to leave, he caught John by the hand and he said, "Promise me Rupert will get his comeuppance."

John gently squeezed his hand. "You can rest assured I will, no matter how long it takes." Whilst they had gone, Sarah and Julie and George went into the kitchen and put the kettle on. Sarah told Julie all that Lord Trelivan had said. "I pray everything will turn out all right for you, but I don't trust that bloody Rupert," Julie said. The tone of her voice got angry at the end of the sentence.

"I see you had a bit of a sparkle in your eye when we got back. What was all that about?" Sarah asked.

"I don't know what you mean," she replied.

"Have you told him how you feel?"

Julie started to blush. "Yes, if you must know," she replied.

"Yes, I must know. Tell me what he said and what you did." Sarah was obviously excited by this.

"Don't you think that's a bit personal?" As Julie spoke, she had the biggest grin you've ever seen.

"It might be personal, but I'm your friend. You should tell me everything." Sarah was teasing, "Now I bet I can make Fred blush', she said.

"Don't you dare," Julie said firmly.

"*"Don't you dare,".* What a voice," said as John and Fred walked through the door.

"Oh, nothing," Julie replied, still blushing.

They sat around the table and ate their Chinese. You didn't have to be a mind-reader to see there was something different with Fred and Julie. They never took their eyes off each other. "What shall we do after tea?" John asked.

"Any suggestions?" Sarah replied.

"Well, I think George might try and let his fox back into the wild tonight." John went on to explain that he had been listening to Miss Pollard, who had rescued many wild animals in her time. She had explained to George that the longer you keep them, the harder it is for them to return. "I just thought if he did, we could all walk up to meet him."

"Do you know where he would let it go?" Fred was quite excited as he asked the question.

"Oh, yes, it'll be in Stony Moor Quarry, that's for sure." John was sounding excited himself.

Stony Moor Quarry was five fields away on the east side of the farmyard. The fields were quite steep and the top field led right to the top of the quarry face. There was a sudden hundred-foot drop in front of you. When you went around the top of the quarry, a gate led on to an old cart track. This led to the other end of the quarry. Half of the quarry was filled with old mine waste, but the track still wound its way to the bottom. Where there was a mine adit going back under the quarry face, the place was teeming with wild life. George spent hours up there, so John knew it was where he'd bring the fox.

George slipped quietly away while the others chatted for about half an hour. "Right then," said John, "let's take a leisurely stroll."

As they opened the gate and walked up the first field,

Julie slipped her hand into Fred's. You could almost feel his smile as he gently squeezed her hand.

"Isn't that sweet?" Julie whispered to John.

"Wonderful," he replied. Quite the romantic is our John. "Steady on," Sarah said, "I'm walking for two, and it's bloody hard work."

They had slowed right down and as they went through the third gate, they were all laughing and joking. As they went through the gate, John looked up across the field. "Shh," he said. There was George coming down across the field, and ten yards behind him was the fox creeping in the grass. Suddenly, there was a large bang. It was a shot from a shotgun. The fox just rolled over. George turned and ran and picked up the dead fox. They all ran over to George. As they got there, Rupert Trelivan arrived at the scene, brandishing a shotgun.

"Get out of my way," he shouted, "I want its tail." He pushed Sarah roughley and she fell back hard on the ground.

John pulled a punch that hit Rupert smack on the nose. "You bastard," he shouted, as he snatched the gun from his hand by the barrels. He smashed the stock hard on the ground with such a force it broke in two. "You're not fit to own a gun," he shouted.

Still holding the gun by the barrels, he threw it as far as he could.

"You'll pay for that," Rupert shouted as he ran to find his gun, clutching his nose.

No one had noticed Sarah lying on the ground. "My God," Julie shouted, "look at Sarah." She was lying on the ground motionless, and there was blood seeping through her skirt.

"O, bloody hell, the baby," John cried. "I'll run for the doctor." Julie had already started to run down the field.

"No, Julie," John replied, "we'll get her in the car and

take her to Tavistock hospital. It'll be much quicker."

He already had her up in his arms. He held her close and tight as he carried her across three fields to the car.

He laid her carefully across the back seat. "I'm coming with you," Julie said. She was already in the car, kneeling down on the floor between the front and back seat, stroking Sarah's forehead.

John looked over to Fred as he got into the car. "Will you look after George?" he shouted.

"Of course," was the reply.

They drove off down the lane at great speed.

In all George's life he had never cried or spoke. But now real tears were flowing down his cheeks, he was swaying back and forward, and as plain as plain could be out of his lips came, "Sarah, Sarah, Sarah."

Fred put his arms around him, his head fell on to Fred's shoulder, and the tears just flowed.

"Come on, George. Let's go get the fox and bury him." He took George by the hand as he spoke.

George never let Fred's hand go, all the way up to the fox. When they got there, Fred picked it up and carried it back down. George stroked its head all the way. "Where shall we bury him?" Fred asked.

George pointed to the garden beside the house. They buried him in front of an old rose bush and then went over to the barn and found some wood and made a cross.

Fred had lost all track of time, but it had become quite dark. He turned to George. "Do you think you should go to bed?"

Once again out of his lips came, "Sarah, Sarah, Sarah."

"Oh, George, she will be so proud of you." Fred led him over to the seat outside the front door. "Now sit down and we'll practice," he said. Fred had this notion that if he said that, he could say anything. After saying Sarah's name a number of times, they went on to John, then Julie, then Fred. He even ended up saying Miss Pollard.

Goodness knows how long they were there, but they both fell fast asleep. Sarah had been kept in hospital and it was the saddest of news; she had lost the baby. It was two a.m. when John and Julie got back to the farm; they found George and Fred asleep. George had his head on Fred's shoulder, and Fred had his head on the tilt, resting on George's head. Julie crept over to Fred and gently shook him. "We're back, Fred," she whispered.

They both woke together. George opened his eyes as he raised his head from Fred's shoulder. To their amazement they heard, "J, J, John, Ju, Ju, Julie." Then without any stuttering, "Fred," he said, as he put his arm around him and cuddled him in. This brought tears to John's eyes. "Did you get him to say that, Fred?" he asked.

"Not really. He said Sarah on his own, then he just sort of got the rest with a bit of practice."

Suddenly, George looked around. He started to get agitated. "Sarah, Sarah, Sarah," he called.

"Come on, George," Fred said, putting his arm around him. "You'll see Sarah tomorrow, but we have to go to sleep first." He led him to his bedroom where he lay on the bed with his clothes on.

Julie had followed them in. "Do you think you should undress him," she asked?

"No, I think we should just let him sleep. He must be shattered, and so must you be," Fred said as he put his arm around her.

John shouted up the stairs, "I've made a cup of tea." They both went down and joined him in the kitchen. It was pretty obvious that he didn't know what to do, and nobody knew what to say. They drank their tea in silence.

Then John suddenly said, "How awful of me, Fred. I

haven't given you a thought. Won't they be worried about you at home?"

"No, don't be so silly," he replied. "I took the liberty to phone my folks to say I won't be home. I'll just sleep down here if that's ok."

"Of course. Are you sure you'll be all right?" John said, sounding very concerned.

"Yes, now go on, get some sleep. You won't be much use to Sarah if you don't get some rest. And the same goes to you, Julie." Fred was sounding quite the authoritarian.

John said good night and went off to bed. Julie came over and kissed Fred on the cheek. "Good night, God bless," she said, as she made her way up the stairs.

Fred settled down in a big old armchair beside the Aga. He had only been there what seemed to be a few minutes when he heard footsteps coming into the room. The curtains were not drawn and the moon shone brightly, lighting up a figure in the doorway. Standing there in a soft, white, thin nightie, that showed every bit of her perfect figure and left nothing to the imagination, stood Julie.

She stretched out her hand. Just as Fred was about to say something, she put her finger to her lips. "Shh," she went as she caught him hold by the hand and led him up the stairs. They just lay on the bed in each other's arms all night.

The next morning, Julie went down and cooked breakfast, but no one seemed hungry. "That old saying things will look better in the morning isn't true," John said. "I still feel as bad as I did last night."

"What time can you visit Sarah?" Fred asked.

"As soon as I like. Sister Blake was an old friend of Sarah's mum's and she's on all weekend. Auntie B, Sarah calls her."

"I'll just go and look at the stock and feed the pigs, and then I'll be off."

"You don't want to be bothered with that," Fred said.

"We'll see to all that. Won't we, Julie."

"I like the we bit," she replied with a smile. "Of course, we will. And don't you worry about George. He'll be fine with us."

"If Sarah can't come home today, I just wonder if George ought to go and see her. It might put his mind at rest." Fred was so concerned about him.

John drank his tea. "Thanks, the pair of you," he said as he went out to the car. "I'll let you know what's happening."

Fred went over to Julie and gave her a kiss. "Love you," he said, then he turned to George. "Come on, you have to show me how to feed the pigs."

You could see George was happy with that. They fed the pigs, then walked up the fields to see the cows and calves. Every time a bird flew by, they would stop. It was like George knew them all personally. On their way back, George kept saying the names he had learnt. Fred thought, "Let's try some more. Trelivan," he kept saying, and it wasn't long before George was repeating it.

As they got back into the yard, Miss Pollard came riding in on her bike. "Hello, Fred," she shouted. "Oh, oh, where's Sarah? Where's Sarah?" she said, looking rather bewildered.

Julie had just come out of the house. "I think you better come in and sit down Miss Pollard," she said. "We have some bad news."

They sat down and told Miss Pollard all about what happened on Saturday night.

"That man he should be strung up. I would like to do it myself," she said, thumping her hand on the table. She went on to say, "Heaven knows what he will get up to now as Lord Trelivan passed away this morning. So he will be lord of the manor. I bet there's a lot of worried people out there."

With that, the phone rang and Julie went off to answer it. While she was gone, George came in from the yard.

"Miss Pollard," he said.

She looked at Fred. "Did I hear right? Did he say that?"

"Oh, yes, he's getting quite clever," Fred replied.

George sat down beside her. "Sarah, Sarah." He had tears in his eyes as he said her name. "Do you think he knows about the baby?" said Miss Pollard, sounding very concerned.

"I think so," Fred replied.

Julie came back into the room. "Good news," she said, "Sarah's coming home this afternoon. Will you stay till they get back, Miss Pollard?"

"Oh, no, dear, but I will come back this afternoon and see her, if you think that will be all right."

"I'm sure it will. Do you want us to tell her about Lord Trelivan, or do you want to when you come back?" asked Julie.

"I would sooner you did, but do it gently, won't you?"

"Of course, we will." Julie sounded very reassuring, and Miss Pollard got up and left.

After she had gone, Fred went over and put his arms around Julie and cuddled her. "Love you," he said.

George, not to be left out, came over with his lovely smile, put his arms around both of them and squeezed his arms tight. They stayed tight together for several moments. I think Fred and Julie were finding it hard to breath.

"I think I'll phone Harold Higgins and tell him I won't be in tomorrow. I think I should stay and help here, don't you, Julie?" Fred said as he broke away from the cuddle.

"I don't expect you will get a very good reception, but I think you're right. They will need a lot of support here, and you're so good with George," she replied.

Fred picked up the phone. As he dialed the number, he was a bit apprehensive at what sort of reception he would get.

An abrupt "yes" came into his ear. "Is that Harold?" Fred asked.

"Who else would it be?" came the reply.

Fred explained what had happened, and how he thought they could do with his help for a couple of days.

Harold replied, "Doesn't matter what other people's problems are, your loyalties should be to me."

Fred went on to say that he had worked for him for four years and had never had a holiday, so could he have some holiday.

"Holidays are for town folk; country folk don't have holidays." Harold was getting cross. You could tell by his voice. "I'll tell you what," he said, "you look after them and I'll look after myself and you needn't bother to come back and that's all I have to say on the matter."

"Well, that suits me," Fred replied as he put the phone down.

Fred went back in to the kitchen. "How did that go?" Julie asked.

"Oh, fine," he quite understood. Fred did not want to worry her. "He told me to take as long as it takes."

"That's good. He has got a human side after all." Julie was interrupted by the sound of a car door. "They're back!" she shouted, quite excited.

John was helping Sarah into the house. George suddenly saw her. "Sarah, Sarah," he said, beaming all over his face.

"Was that you, George?" she asked. As she looked at him, tears flowed down her cheeks. He came right over and put his arms around her.

"I've made up your bed and I found some extra pillows in your airing cupboard, so I put them on the bed, as well," Julie said as she was taking the kettle off the Aga and pouring the water into the tea pot. "Do you want to go up to bed and I'll bring a cuppa up?" Julie was feeling so concerned, but didn't know what to say.

Sarah realised this. "Oh, Julie dear, it's nice of you to fuss, but I think I'll sit down here in the armchair."

As she sat in the chair, there was some other bad news. "I don't know if now is the time to tell you, but I promised Miss Pollard I would before she comes around."

"I know what it is. He was in hospital when he died. Auntie B told me, two deaths on the same day," Sarah said as she tried to hold back the emotion. But she could hold it no longer. "Why did I lose my baby?" she cried. "Why my baby?" she repeated.

"There, there, now," John said as he sat down on the floor beside her and gently stroked her forehead.

"Thanks for what you and Fred are doing," Sarah said. She reached out over John and caught hold of Julie's hand, as she brought the tea around. "They told me it's unusual to abort at seven months, you know." It seemed that talking about it was helping Sarah. "You're all wonderful," she said. Then there was a pause and tears started to flow again. "I wish my mum was here; she would know what to do."

"It's me," a voice came from the door. Fred, John, Julie and George all said in perfect harmony, "Miss Pollard."

"That's right, dears, it's me, come to see the sick."

"Sit down here beside Sarah," John said as he got up from the floor and pulled a chair from the table and placed beside her armchair. Now, dear, how are you going to manage, as you have to rest? You know I'll come and do what I can, but I don't know how I'll be tied up at the big house."

John said, "Oh, don't worry about us. Julie is staying with us until she gets married." He was rather bemused when Julie kicked him in the shin. "What was that for?" he whispered.

Julie, trying to change the subject, blurted out, "Mr Higgins has told Fred he can help as long as it takes."

But that didn't work. Miss Pollard turned to Julie. "Your

man has gone to work at Riddle Down farm, they tell me. It's the biggest dairy farm in the southwest, you know. It was so lucky that there were two jobs going there and they both got them. It belongs to my second cousin Bill Hambley. That's how I know all this; see, dear, it's a small world."

Julie looked surprised. "What do you mean both?" she said.

"You know, one for his friend, Julian Sleep. He has a job there as well. Apparently they both worked together at Mill Farm and were friends."

Miss Pollard turned to Sarah. "Hark at me going on. It's you I came to see, dear, now how are you feeling? Is there anything I can do before I rush off?"

Miss Pollard left. "Are you going to stay here with us tonight Fred?" Sarah asked. "We would like you to stay; Julie will make up the bed in the front room."

"I will have to go home and get some clean clothes, but yes, I'd love to stay."

George, who had just been sitting there, looked up at hearing this. "Fred," he said. You could tell he approved.

"Can I ride back with you when you go for your clothes? I have something to tell my parents." Julie then turned to Sarah and said, "It won't be necessary to make up the spare bed. He can share with me."

This was the first time Sarah smiled since she came home! "What, you mean ..." she said, quite excited.

"Yes," Julie replied.

"What's going on?" John asked. "Am I missing something?"

"Oh, nothing for you to worry about. You go out and look at your cows and just let me and Julie have a chat a minute."

The three men went out and walked over to the baby pigs. "Nature is cruel sometimes," John said as he put his head in his hands. "Here's a pig with eleven piglets and they all survived, and we can't keep one baby alive." He took a hanky out of his pocket and wiped his eyes. "I try to keep my emotions back when I'm around Sarah, but God, it's bloody hard."

Over in the house, Sarah was questioning Julie. "You told him how you felt? What did he say? Are you excited?"

"Yes, I told him and he said he loves me, and I just know he does. And I know I love him and I want to spend all my time with him."

"Where did this happen?"

"In the meadow with all the wild flowers."

"Oh, how romantic. I'm so delighted for you. Have you told Robert?"

"No, I want Fred to drive me up there, and I will tell him to his face, not over the phone."

"You seemed surprised when Miss Pollard said that someone had gone with him. Who was it?" she asked.

"Julian Sleep."

"Did you know him?" Sarah was getting inquisitive.

"Yes, I know him. He's Robert's big drinking partner. I'm not surprised he didn't tell me. He knows I wouldn't approve; that's why I agreed to move up there. I thought things would be different if he was away from Julian."

"Oh, well, I think how things have turned out are the best for you," Sarah said as her eyes started to fill with tears. For just a few minutes her mind had been taken off her troubles.

"Oh, poor you." Julie put her arm around her shoulder as she spoke. "I just don't know what to say. I feel so helpless."

"You just being here does help more than you know."

With that, the phone rang. "Do you want me to answer that?" Julie asked.

"Please," Sarah nodded.

Julie returned to the room and whispered, "It's the vicar. He wants to come around seven thirty tonight. What shall I tell him?"

"You better tell him yes, we have to see him some time and I've got some questions for him."

"Look, I'll go out and get John, and me and Fred can go and get his stuff and we'll come back when the vicar has gone."

Julie went out in the yard and found all three of them over by the pigs. "I think you should go in with Sarah, John, she needs you. Oh, and by the way, the vicar is coming at seven thirty."

"I should go up and see the cows first," John replied. Fred quickly came in. "Don't worry about that. Julie and I will walk up and see them before we go."

John's eyes just filled up. "What it is to have friends like you. Come on, George, I'm sure Sarah will want you there as well."

Fred and Julie walked up across the fields arm in arm until they came to the field with the cows. In they walked around the field and looked at every cow.

As they came along the top of the field, there was an old stone barn. "What's in there?" Julie asked.

"How would I know?" Fred replied jokingly.

"Come on, let's have a look. It looks so quaint," Julie said as she pulled Fred over to the door and pushed it open. The barn was empty except for about two feet of hay all over the floor.

With their arms around each other, they flopped down on the hay.

Fred started to put his fingers through her hair. They looked deep in to each other's eyes, then kissed passionately.

Fred suddenly pushed away. "What's wrong?" Julie couldn't understand why he had pushed her away. "Have I done something wrong?"

"No, no, you could never do anything wrong. It's me. I haven't been exactly honest with you."

"What do you mean? Is there someone else?" she asked, although she couldn't see how there could be.

"Nothing like that. I didn't tell you because I didn't want to worry. You know the phone call I made to Harold Higgins? Well, he didn't understand. He said that John and Sarah's problems weren't his. He basically told me not to come back."

"Oh, I do love you," she replied in a soft voice, and she whispered in his ear, "I want you to make love to me now."

She stood up and slowly unbuttoned her dress down the front. When she had undone the last button, she slowly pushed it off her shoulders, letting it drop to the floor. She had a low-cut red bra that showed firm breasts with deep cleavage and a skimpy pair of pants to match.

Fred could not take his eyes off her. She was a real thing of beauty. She put her hands around her back to undo her bra.

"Stop." Fred got up from the hay. "Let me," he whispered as he put his arms around her, and he undid the clasp as if it was something he had done a hundred times before.

They both collapsed back on the hay and made love slowly and passionately.

After they had made love, they both lay back on the hay. Julie suddenly turned towards Fred. "What are you going to do?" she asked.

"What do you mean?" Fred said in a surprised voice.

"Well, if you don't have a job."

"Don't worry about me. I don't spend much. I've saved quite a bit since I started work, so I'll be alright for a week or two."

Julie was now sounding worried. "Perhaps John and Sarah will give you a job."

"No, their money is quite tight, and who knows what will happen now that Rupert will inherit. Anyway, I might want to do something different."

"Like what?" she asked.

"Well," he replied, "I love farming and the animals, and I know we have only been coming here a couple of weeks, but I have built up a close relationship with George."

Fred was sounding very serious and concerned as he continued, "George has had a lot of sorrow at the moment, but his life generally is quite good, on the whole. He is deeply loved by John, Sarah and the people around him, but I keep thinking there must be people like George that aren't so lucky and I would just like to do something to help them."

"Like what?" Julie was getting interested.

"Oh, I don't know. Start a charity that offers short breaks for them, just something that will give them a better way of life, something to live for."

Julie put her arms around him. "Oh, I do love you," she said, hugging him as tight as she could. "Am I part of this plan of yours?" she continued.

Fred pushed her back gently. He cupped his hands around her face and looked deeply into her eyes. "It's just a dream I have, and you're always in my dreams." He bent forward and kissed her gently.

"Come on," Fred said, getting up and making himself presentable. "We have to go and get my clothes."

"I prefer you without them," came the reply, with a large smile.

"God, you look beautiful when you smile," Fred said. He had the most contented look on his face.

"Only when I smile?" Julie said, as she put her dress on over her shoulders and started to do the buttons up. As they left the shed, they caught hold hands and ran down across the fields to the car.

They drove off, he to get his clothes and Julie to tell her mother that the wedding was off. Fred soon got a few clothes together. He told his parents all about what had happened. His mother was a very caring person; you could tell where Fred got it from.

"Don't worry, love, something will turn up," she said as he went out of the door. It was taking longer for Julie to tell her mum. It seemed that Fred was waiting for ages. She suddenly appeared and jumped in the car.

"How did that go?" Fred asked.

"Not as bad as I thought. In fact. Mum was quite understanding. She said if it's not right, it's no good going ahead with it. But I also had the third degree, what a good boy he was and all that."

When they got back to the farmyard, there was a car parked outside the back door. "The vicar is still here. We ought not to go in yet," Fred said.

"I know," Julie said, "let's walk down to the pub and have a quick drink. Our little celebration."

The vicar was having quite a job on his hands trying to comfort Sarah.

"Why did my baby die?" she kept asking. "Why my baby?"

"I don't know why God moves in what we think strange ways." The vicar was trying hard to explain. "We know God loves us all," he continued. "How or why he chooses a special few we will never know, but we do know the ones he chooses are special."

Sarah looked at him, wiping the tears from her eyes. "My mum was special," she said, "Really special. And my baby would have been special, too."

The vicar smiled at her. "I knew your mother well. She

was a very special woman. I would go further than that," he said. "She was the most caring woman you could ever wish to know. It was easy to see why God picked her. If I was God, I would have wanted her as an angel."

"Now, my dears," he said as he stood up making his way out, "I'll come and see you again about the funeral arrangements, and don't forget, my door is open any time. Now. God bless you both."

"Thanks a lot for coming. You've helped a lot," Sarah said as she leaned towards him and kissed his cheek.

After quite an eventful hour down the pub, Fred and Julie returned as the vicar was leaving.

When they had arrived at the at the pub (The Butcher's Arms), they were greeted by a cheerful, smiling face. "Good evening. And what can I get you?" asked the smiling face. Fred looked at Julie. "Babysham, is it?" he asked.

Julie just nodded. She couldn't take her eyes off the way the pub was done out. Down the middle of the pub was a thick beam with a row of butcher's hooks, and some had joints of meat hanging from them; some had rabbits, then there were pheasants and pigeons, and a few were empty.

"Don't worry, dear," said the voice behind the bar, "the birds and rabbits are stuffed and the meat is plastic. Now then, Babysham, was it?"

"Oh yes, and a pint of best, please." Fred was looking at the characters in the pub.

"You're the two friends of John and Sarah, aren't you?" the smiling voice asked, as he drew the pint out of a barrel which was one of many lined up at the back of the bar. As he turned and put the drinks in front of them, he put out his hand. "I'm Ben, by the way."

Fred shook him by the hand and introduced them both. It was a real, firm shake. "Sad business about the baby. Lovely girl, that Sarah. She doesn't deserve that. Will you pass on our condolences?"

You could tell Ben was sincere. "It's a bit solemn in here tonight with the death of Lord Trelivan. People are worried about what is going to happen next."

Suddenly the door burst open and in came Rupert Trelivan. "What do you want?" asked Ben, the landlord, angrily, you know you're not welcome here.

"Careful what you say, landlord," he replied. "don't forget who's your landlord. Oh, and look who's here. It's the friends of the slut and her half wit brother. Where are they, home packing?"

He looked around the pub. "Look at Farmer Jones over there. He couldn't pay last quarter rent 'cause my daddy said he had poorly cows. Oh, what a shame," he said sarcastically. "You better pay this quarter, or you're out on your ear. There's no more charity on this estate, now I'm Lord."

With that, a rather large man who had been sitting in the corner got up and walked towards Rupert. He was about six feet tall and looked three feet wide. "You can take back what you called Sarah and her brother," he said, his face just inches away from Rupert's.

"Don't you want to keep your blacksmith's shop?" Rupert asked threateningly. "The girl's a slut, just like her mother," he continued.

Rupert was wearing a three-quarter-length suede coat with a white fur collar. The blacksmith, who they called Cart, after a carthorse, picked Rupert up by his lapels and hung him by his collar on one of the meat hooks that were hanging from the beam. "Now, let me tell you something, you little runt." Cart was all fired up. "When I broke my leg, that girl's mother brought me dinner every day. You see Jim over there in the corner? When his mother was dying, she sat with her every night. There's not one person in this village that Molly Page didn't show some kindness to. She was a true lady, an angel to a lot of people. So you can stay up there until I hear you take those words back."

Fred turned to Cart and shook him by the hand. "It's been a real pleasure to meet you," he said. "I'd like to stay for more, but we really must get back to John and Sarah."

"Give them my love," he replied in a soft voice. Then, across the pub, in almost perfect harmony came, "And ours, too."

Fred and Julie ran back laughing to the farm. Sarah was still in the doorway after seeing the vicar off.

"What have you two been up to?" she asked.

"Let's go inside, and we'll tell you all about it. It might just make you smile," Julie said, as she put her arm around her and led her to the kitchen.

They all sat down around the kitchen table, and Julie told them all about what happened in the pub.

"I would love to have seen that." It was nice to see a smile on Sarah's face. Even George found it funny. I don't know if he understood or not.

Fred came in to the conversation. "There was one thing that was quite clear tonight; the love in the village for you and the love they had for your mum is totally out of this world."

Smiles didn't last long, as Sarah said, "Do you think things like what happened down the pub and us laughing at them make us bad people? Is that why God punishes us?"

"My dear Sarah," Julie put her hands across the table and caught hold her hands, then she continued. "Now what did the vicar say? I bet he didn't say you were a bad person. Neither did anyone down the village."

"Now come on, you mustn't think like that. God tries to watch over us all the time, but sometimes he gets caught up with other people and just for a moment he takes his eye off us. He will return our loved ones to us, trust me. I believe you will meet your baby. Even if it is just her spirit, she will bring her love."

"How will I know when the spirit comes?"

"Oh, you will know all right, there will be no mistaking her."

"How do you know all these things? Are they really true?"

"I had a very wise Nan. She told me, she used to say, "When I die, don't think you have got rid of me." Not long after she died we had a stray cat come in. She is still home now. And I know that cat is my Nan."

"My dear Julie," Sarah replied, "you always say the nicest things, and what you say does help. Now give us a cuddle and let's all get to bed."

"Is it all right if I have a bath?" Fred asked.

"Of course. We'll go on to bed, then you can help yourself," Sarah replied.

"The bathroom is downstairs. It's a small room built on the side of the house, with just a wash basin and a large cast iron bath with two large brass taps on one end. I'll go and run your water," Julie said as she left room. "I'll give you a shout when it's ready." She was gone about five minutes, then suddenly Fred heard, "It's ready."

He went in to the bathroom and, much to his surprise, there was Julie lying in the bath. "Come on, jump in," she said. "I've got the tap end."

Fred was rather embarrassed. You could tell he didn't know what to say.

Julie stood up and got out of the bath. She put her arms around him. "I'm so sorry," she said. "The last thing I wanted was to embarrass you. I thought you would enjoy it."

"Oh, trust me," Fred said, "anywhere else and I would; but it's just that it's someone else's house and what they've been through – it doesn't seem right."

"Sorry," she said again, "I'll go on to bed and leave you

to your bath." Fred had his bath and went to the bedroom. Julie was lying in bed. It was obvious she had been crying. "What's wrong?" Fred asked.

"I've upset you. It was so thoughtless. What do you think of me?"

"Now, let me see. What do I think of you?" He put his arms around her. "I think you are the most beautiful thing I know; I think you're the kindest person I know, I think you're the most gracious person I know. I also know I want to spend the rest of my life with you."

She snuggled into his chest, all content. "Love you," she said.

They soon fell asleep.

The next morning, they all sat down to breakfast. No one was hungry or knew what to say. Sarah was the first to break the ice. "When do you think you will go and see Robert?" she asked Julie.

"There's no rush," Julie replied as she picked up her knife and fork. She just moved her breakfast around the plate.

The sooner you do it, the better, if you ask me. The longer you delay, the harder it'll be. Sarah put the men's breakfasts down in front of them, then got her own and sat down by Julie. "I don't know why I cooked this. I don't want it." She started to cry.

Julie put her arm around her. "Come on, you should still be in bed, not down here cooking breakfast. You need rest."

"That's what I told her," John said, "but she won't listen to me."

"Oh, I would sooner be out doing something. I need to keep busy. You haven't answered my question. When are you going to tell Robert?"

"As I said, no hurry." It was obvious Julie just wanted to put it off for as long as possible.

"If I was you, I'd get Fred to drive you there today and get it over with."

"I don't want to leave you alone, if John's out working." Julie was sounding genuinely concerned.

John looked over to Julie. "Sarah is right. You should go. I won't leave her alone, and we have to see the undertaker and get the death certificate."

Sarah tried hard to hold back the tears, but they just flowed and flowed.

"Come now," John said as he put his arms around her, "would you like Julie to stay here and I go and do it on my own?"

"No, I want to come. They said I could see my baby. I want to see her one last time."

"Oh, Sarah dear, I didn't realise you could see the baby. I just thought … I don't know what I thought. I feel so awful."

Julie was so upset to think she hadn't realised the baby was fully grown, she ran out of the room crying.

Fred got up to go after her. Sarah put her one hand on Fred's arm and wiped her eyes with the other. "Let me go," she said quietly.

Sarah found Julie lying on the bed, crying. She sat down on the bed beside her and started to stroke her head. "Come on, now, don't upset yourself like this," she said, as she started to dry Julie's eyes with her hanky.

"I feel so bad. I just couldn't picture it as a real baby," she said.

"She was a real baby all right; they said I was very unlucky; the fall must have killed her. I must have fallen heavy on her; she wouldn't have just aborted at seven and half months." Sarah seemed more relaxed as she was trying to explain things to Julie. "We are going to give her a name and we are going to call her after you, if that's all right."

"Of course, it's all right. I'd consider it an honour," Julie said as she sat up and dried her eyes.

— 39 —

"Now, come on, you and Fred go and see that old boyfriend of yours, and John and I will go and do what we have too."

As Fred and Julie were about to leave, a car pulled into the yard. Two men in pinstriped suits got out and walked over to the door. They got to the door just as Julie was leaving. "Mrs Brite?" one asked.

"Oh, no, that's not me," she replied and shouted in to Sarah. As Sarah approached the door, "This is her," Julie blurted out. She wasn't used to seeing men in suits.

The two men introduced themselves. "I'm Mr Starkey, and this is Mr Knight. We are solicitors of the late Lord Trelivan. May we come in?" he asked.

"As long as you haven't come to kick us out," Sarah replied.

"Nothing like that, my dear," they replied.

"Are we all right in here?" Sarah asked as she led them in to the kitchen (this seems to be the only room used on the farm). "Shall I get my husband?"

"Yes, if you wish. It might be better if you were both here," said the second man, who was Mr Knight and much softer spoken. The two solicitors sat opposite John and Sarah at the kitchen table.

Mr Knight looked at them. "First, let me offer our sincere condolences on the death of your baby."

He continued. "As you are aware, Lord Trelivan has passed away. Now, in normal circumstances, we would read the will after the funeral, and we promised Lord Trelivan we would do this."

Mr Starkey came in. "He wanted it done in the pub."

"That's right," Mr Knight continued, "under the circumstances we have taken advice from the lord chief justice, and it has been decided to hold the reading of the will before the funereal, and this will take place on Wednesday night at The Butcher's Arms."

"Can you tell us why?" John asked.

"Afraid not," Mr Starkey replied, "but it will all be made clear on that night."

Mr Knight got up. "Now, don't worry, my dears, we have to go. We have other people to see, and God bless you both," he said as he reached out and shook their hands across the table.

"What a nice man that Mr Knight seems. I wonder what it's all about? And why come and see us?" The suspense was almost too much for Sarah.

"You shouldn't read too much into it," John replied. "With a bit of luck he's tied it up so that Rupert can't kick us out. And I expect it's the same for the others he has to see."

Fred and Julie drove off to Oakhampton, wondering who the two men were. It had completely taken Julie's mind off why she was going to Oakhampton. "Do you know where the farm is?" Julie asked.

"How the hell would I know?" Fred replied.

"All right, keep your shirt on." She could tell he was getting anxious for her. "Miss Pollard said you turn right at the top of the hill," Fred said much more calmly.

"Oh, look, there's a sign: Riddle Down pedigree Frisians. That's it," Julie shouted. She looked at Fred. "I want to go home now. I don't know if I can do this. Perhaps it would be better if I went back and wrote him a letter."

Fred stopped the car just down the road. There were two cottages standing on their own further down the road. You could see the start of the farm.

Fred put his arm around her. "I would think it's one of those cottages," he said. "Now, you don't have to do this. But if you don't, you might regret it when we get back."

"You'll wait for me," she said as she got out of the car.

"Of course, I will. Where do you think I'm going, silly," he replied.

Julie walked down the road to the cottages. Fred could see her put her hand up to the glass and look through the windows as she went by. He lost sight of her as she went in around the back. It was only a matter of moments before she came running up the road, crying.

Fred quickly jumped out of the car and ran down the road to meet her. "What's wrong? What's wrong?" he shouted.

"Get me in the car; I feel sick," she cried.

They got back in the car. "Now, whatever is wrong?" Fred said. "Has he done something to you?"

"Just start the car and get out of here, or I just don't know what I'll do. I could kill the bastard." Fred had never seen Julie like this before.

They had just left Oakhampton and started to come across Dartmoor. "Stop the car," Julie shouted. "Stop the car, I want to be sick."

Fred quickly pulled onto the moor; Julie got out and started purging.

Fred got out and put his arm around her. "Now, whatever is it?" he asked.

She turned to him. "Hold me," she said, "hold me tight."

Fred pulled her tight in to his body.

"The bastard was with someone else. They were naked on the settee when I looked through the window."

Fred released his grip gently and looked down at her. "I can understand how you could be a bit surprised, but you say you have no feelings for him. I don't see the problem, and I'm a bit bewildered, to say the least, as to why you are so upset," he said.

"I'm mad," she replied. "Trust me, I'm mad."

"So explain it to me, then." Fred was sounding cross.

"The bastard was with a man. I could except it if he was with a woman, but not this. The bastard's a queer. No wonder he never touched me, and thank God he didn't. Just

— *42* —

to think I've kissed him makes me feel sick."

Fred pulled her tight in to his body, so tight that every bit of their bodies touched. They stayed close together for several minutes. She looked up at him, stood on tiptoe and kissed him passionately. Her face turned to a smile. "I hope you've got no surprises for me," she said.

"No surprises. What you see is what you get. Now come on, let's get back," Fred said as he opened the car door.

Julie put her hand on his and looked passionately into his eyes and said, "You know that shed with the hay in it at top of the field?"

"How could I forget it?" he replied.

"Will you take me there tonight?" Julie was now sounding excited.

"You try and stop me," he replied, as he leaned forward and kissed her gently on her lips.

They soon got back in the yard. George was in the yard to greet them. "Fred, Fred," he shouted.

Sarah appeared at the door. "You'd better go with him; he's been waiting to show you something. And you, missy, can come and tell me all about your day."

Julie and Sarah went indoors, and Fred and George went up the granite steps to the barn. As they opened the door, George put his finger to his lips. They went in quietly, and there on the beam in front of them was a beautiful white owl. Its feathers were as white as snow. George took Fred by the arm and led him to two sacks of corn in the corner of the barn and they sat on one each.

Julie and Sarah were sat at the kitchen table. "Now tell me, Julie dear, what Robert said."

"He didn't say anything. He didn't have a chance; he just made me feel sick."

"How do you mean?"

"I mean the bastard's a queer."

Sarah started to laugh. "How do you know? What did he say?"

"I know because I saw them naked on the settee. It would make anyone sick, let alone an ex-girlfriend."

"There might be a perfect explanation."

"Take it from me – what I saw needs no explanation."

"Surely you must have had some idea. I think I would have known if John was like that." Sarah was somewhat surprised, to say the least.

"I just can't get it out of my mind. Animals don't even behave like that. It makes me sick; the bastard should be shot." Julie was getting quite wound up. "I know now that's why he never touched me," she continued. "He kept saying we should save it until we get married. My God, what would have happened if we did get married? Don't laugh at me." Julie looked across at Sarah and could see she was finding it hard not to laugh, but she could hold it back no longer. She just roared with laughter, and Julie joined her.

"There, do you feel better now?" Sarah asked.

"Yes, thanks for that. You might think I'm stupid. Its ages since Robert kissed me, but all the way back in the car I kept wiping my mouth. I wanted Fred to kiss me. I thought it would take it away. Now, tell me all about the men in the suits and how your day went."

Sarah sat down and told her all about the suits, and then she started to break down. "We can't arrange the funeral yet, as the undertakers have to wait for Lord Trelivan's arrangements to be made. And they can't do that until after Wednesday. I do wonder what it's all about."

"Look at the time," Sarah said, wiping the tears from her eyes. She got up and reached for the kettle. "I must think about getting the tea."

"Why don't you sit down and let me do it? You know you

should be resting. You will make yourself ill if you don't rest."

"Oh, no, I want to keep busy. It helps better than any rest. Besides, making a few sandwiches is not exactly hard work. You go and see what Fred and George are up to."

"I'll go and get them." Julie got up and kissed her on the cheek as she ran out the door.

She could see the barn door was open. She ran up the steps and stopped suddenly when she got to the door. She stood there for a few moments just watching. "I'm so lucky," she thought, "to have someone so kind loving and thoughtful. I just want to hug and hug him." Fred was sat on one sack, looking at George on another. He kept saying, "Owl, Owl, Owl," and George kept trying to repeat it.

Julie came into the barn. "What are you two up to?" she shouted.

George looked at her and pointed to the beam. "Owl," he said.

"He's got it," Fred said, with a tone of satisfaction in his voice.

George went out of the barn, excited. "Sarah, Owl," he said as he went out the door.

"He's going to tell Sarah about the Owl," Julie said as she put her arm around Fred. "Oh, I do love you, Freddy kindness."

John drove into the yard as they came down the steps. He had just come back from the mill with some pig meal for the pigs.

"You go on in and I'll give John a hand unloading a minute," Fred said as he picked up a sack from the pickup.

After they had unloaded, they went in for tea. During tea, the topic of conversation was all about what the solicitors had said and all sorts of speculation. "Fred and I were thinking of going out for a walk after tea." Julie had an air of excitement in her voice.

"What a good idea," Sarah replied. "You can come back via the pub and see what the gossip is down there."

"I think I'll just go and change, if we are going down the pub." Julie rushed up the stairs.

"What's got her all excited?" John put his arms around Sarah as he said it. "Did I ever get you excited like that?" he asked with a smile.

"Oh, you still do, dear, you still do," she repeated quietly as her eyes filled with tears.

Julie came back down into the kitchen. Her mood changed when she saw Sarah crying. "Oh, come, Sarah," she went over and put her arms around both of them, "we won't go out we'll stay here with you, won't we Fred."

Sarah wiped her eyes. "Oh, yes, you must go out. I want to know what everyone is saying."

"Are you still going for a walk?" John asked.

"Oh, yes, if you're sure you don't mind."

"It's just that I don't see many walkers in a tight pair of pants like that." Julie just poked her tongue out at him and smiled. (But she did look beautiful.)

"Come on then, Fred, let's go and get some news."

They walked out of the gate that led up to the field where the shed was. They walked up across the field with their arms around each other.

"Fred, would you mind if when we get to the shed we don't make love?" Julie was sounding all emotional.

"Of course not. We don't have to go to the shed; it was your idea any way."

"I know it was and I want to go in there and lay on the hay and have you hold me as tight as you can. I just want to be in your arms."

"That'll do for me," Fred replied.

They soon got to the shed and flopped down on the hay. They just lay there cuddled in each other's arms; neither one of them spoke for ages.

Julie broke the silence. "I love you, and this place, and I think I'm the luckiest person in the world."

"And what makes you say that? I might be the luckiest." Fred was teasing her.

"No, I'm definitely the luckiest. I could have married a queer." Julie's mood was beginning to change.

"Now, come on, don't upset yourself again over it. As you said, you are lucky you didn't get married. Some people can't help the way there made." Fred was trying to reassure her.

"That's typical of you; you always see the good in people. But do you know what really pisses me off? It's the fact that he knows it's wrong and he chose to use me for a smoke screen, and even now he's spoiling my night."

"Come here and give me a kiss, and it'll make it all better." Fred pulled her close to him and their lips met.

The kiss lasted for minutes. As they broke away, she whispered, "I'm so sorry."

"What are you sorry about?" Fred was puzzled.

"You know, sorry that I dragged you up here and then I didn't want to do it."

Fred laughed. "You are a silly sausage. Just being here with you is contentment for me. Anyway, I would be tired out if I had to get those tight jeans off you."

"Don't you like them?"

"More than that – I love them," Fred had a large smile on his face as he said it.

"I worry sometimes, you know," Julie was sounding serious.

"What about?"

"Well, you know, when we do it, do I do it right?" Julie was starting to embarrass Fred.

"Why? Is there a wrong way?" he replied. "Now come on, enough of this talk. Let's go for that drink."

"I do love you, my Freddy kindness." Julie put her arm around him and they walked down to the pub. She was feeling full of contentment.

The talk in the pub was all speculation about the will. "Do John and Sarah know what it's all about?" Ben the landlord asked.

"They don't know any more than you do," Fred said, as he ordered their drinks.

"Don't see Miss Pollard around. I bet she knows." I think Ben was more curious than anyone.

Cart the blacksmith came over. "It's no good to speculate; there is only one thing that is certain. We won't benefit, the Lord will be missed, and our lives will be a lot worse when that son of his inherits."

"You never said truer words, Cart. You always speak a lot of sense," Ben said as he walked to the other end of the bar to serve someone else.

Cart stayed and talked with Fred and Julie. There was a lot of talk about what they each did and how they became friends with Sarah and John.

About an hour had passed when Julie said, "We better be getting back. I don't like to think of them there too long. I think when we are there it takes their minds off it for a while."

"I see you are a couple of good kids," Cart said. "Give them my love, I feel guilty not going up to see them, but I never know if people coming makes it better or worse."

"Good night, good night," they all shouted as they left the pub.

"Nice people, aren't they," Julie said as they walked back up the road.

Fred replied, "Full of wisdom. I think it's because the village is part of the estate. It's like a big family, with Lord Trelivan as the father."

"God, he'll be missed. What will those people do when Rupert runs things? And Sarah and John come to that." Julie was quite concerned about her friends.

As they got back into the yard, George was leaning on the gate. "What are you up to, George?" He was smiling all over. "Owl, owl, owl," he said, pointing to the electric pole in the corner of the yard. There, perched on top, was the owl.

"I could cuddle him when he smiles like that."

"Hey, that's enough of that, Jew, you'll make me jealous," Fred said, with a smile as big as George's.

"Are you coming in, George?" they asked as they went over to the door.

George shook his head. Fred and Julie went on in.

As they walked into the kitchen, you could just feel the sadness. "Hi, we're back," Julie shouted trying to lift the spirits. You could see the smiles that came back were make-believe.

"What's the news?" Sarah asked, her eyes red. You could tell there had been a lot of tears.

"No news; plenty of speculation, though." Julie went over and put her arms around Sarah as she answered. "Sarah, love, you look absolutely shattered. Why don't you go on to bed."

"I have to see to George. He will want some supper before he goes to bed," she replied.

"Don't be so silly. I'll look after George. Now, off you go, and you John." Julie was being quite the authoritarian.

Sarah and John went on to bed. "I'll go out and see George while you get him some supper," Fred said as he walked towards the door.

George was still watching the owl. It was almost as if he the owl knew it. He kept flying off and hovering over the yard, then flying back to the post.

"You coming in for supper now, George?" he asked.

He nodded in reply.

They got into the kitchen just as Julie put the toast down on the table. "You look contented with yourself," she said, with a big smile on her face.

They ate their toast and had their drinks. George couldn't stop saying owl.

"You love that. It's made your day, hasn't it," Julie said to Fred.

"I think he can say a lot more. I'd like to think I can get him to talk properly," Fred said, with a look of satisfaction on his face. "Are we all ready for bed? I'll lock the back door. I think we can all do with a good night's sleep." Fred went and locked the door, and they all went to bed.

The next morning they were all sitting down having breakfast. "What's everyone doing today?" Sarah asked. "I think you three men should go out and do something around the farm, and Julie and I should have a good old natter. Just try to get some normality, try to take our mind off things." With that, Sarah's eyes just filled up. "If that's possible," she continued.

"I think we should go and take the gate posts out up at the corn fields. Bill Tucker got a new combine with a twelve foot cut, and it won't go through the gate." John was trying to put a brave face on.

"That's sorted, then," Julie said, "because I've got something to talk to Sarah about." Off the three men went and Julie and Sarah did the breakfast dishes.

"Now that the dishes are out of the way, what did you want to talk to me about?" Sarah said as she sat down in the chair at one end of the table and Julie at the other.

"It's a bit personal."

"Oh, really. How personal?" Sarah asked.

"Very personal," came the reply.

"Go on, then," Sarah said, "try me."

"Well," Julie was thinking of her words carefully, "it's no good beating about the bush," she said. "Do you enjoy sex?"

"What a question!" Sarah was blushing, but gave a straight answer.

"Of course, I do. Why, don't you?" she replied.

"Oh, yes, very much," Julie replied. "I say very much, but I've only done it twice. How do I know if I've done it right?"

"Is there a right way and a wrong way?" Sarah was laughing at her.

"Oh, don't make fun of me. I'm nearly twenty and have no experience with life. Don't you think that's sad?" Julie said with a glum face.

"Far from it. I think it's something to be proud of, especially if you saved yourself for Mr Right." Sarah was reassuring her.

"You think? So how do you explain this? Last night I asked him to go somewhere special and make love to me. When we got there, I just wanted him to hold me. I didn't want to do it, but he didn't complain, he didn't try anything; he just held me, and my whole body just tingled with excitement. Afterward I kept thinking, why didn't he try to make love? Is it because I'm no good at it? Perhaps he didn't enjoy it when we did it."

"My dear Julie, did it not occur to you that it's because he loves and respects you? That's why he went along with your wish." Sarah continued, "My mother gave me great advice. I asked her questions like you asked me once. She said, when you have sex you do as little or as much as you both feel comfortable with. When two people really love each other, making love is wonderful. She always told me not to confuse making love with lust. So I think that will answer all your questions. You have found real love."

"I wish I had met your mum. She sounds wonderful."

Julie's face was much happier now. "She was, and I do miss her. Now, put the kettle on or you will start my waterworks off." Sarah was holding back the tears. "We'll have a cup of tea and then shall we make pasties for dinner? It doesn't matter what time they come back, they can have them hot or cold."

"Good idea. Fred loves a pasty," Julie said. "Even better if the Aga cooks them I expect," they both smiled.

They drank their tea, and Sarah went to the fridge to get the meat. "That's strange; the meat's gone. I must be losing my marbles. I could have sworn I bought some on Friday."

"Never mind. With all that's going on, perhaps you forgot," Julie was comforting her. "Shall we walk down the village and get some? They could have them for tea then."

"Oh, Julie dear, I don't want to meet people yet. But would you mind going? You could get five chops, as well, that will do for tomorrow."

"I won't be long." Julie ran down and back so as not to leave Sarah alone for long.

The three men were out in the corn fields making the gateways wide enough for the combine. George was wandering around everywhere; the birds were following him and singing. It was a glorious summer day. George came running up to John and started pulling on his arm and pointing across the field.

"What is it?" John asked.

"I think we better go with him and look," Fred said, wiping the sweat from his brow. They walked up across the field, and there out in the middle were two men. One had a theodolite he was looking through, the other was writing down things.

They walked across the field to meet the two men. "Can I help you?" John said. "Can I ask who you are and what you are doing?"

"We are surveyors, and we are surveying this land," the man that was taking notes replied.

"I don't know who gave you permission or what you are surveying for, but you are trespassing and I must ask you to leave," John said sternly.

The man got out a letter and ordnance survey map from his bag. He studied it for a few seconds. "No, we are definitely in the right place," he said, "Look." He produced a letter from Rupert Trelivan plus the ordnance survey map with a circle around the farm.

"Now, if you don't mind, we have to get on as we have to get the planning application for the golf course in by Friday."

"I'm sorry, but you can't continue, and you will have to leave. I am the tenant and you can't do this without my permission." John was pointing to the gate.

"We have been working on this for months," the man replied. "I don't think Mr Trelivan will be very happy." He started to put his equipment away.

"Just a minute," Fred piped in. He pulled John to one side. "Do you think it's wise? If you turn them off, you know who will come around presently and upset Sarah. I know how mad you are feeling, but them surveying won't make any difference, whatever happens."

"No, you're right. They may just as well carry on. We can sort it out later." John went back to the men and told them to carry on.

He turned to Fred. "Thanks for that. I don't think we should mention it to Sarah until after tomorrow."

"I agree," Fred nodded in reply.

"I think we have done enough for today. My mind's not on it. I'll be glad when we can make the funeral arrangements. Come on, let's go back to the house. There are jobs we can do around the yard." You could tell John wanted to be close to Sarah.

"With a bit of luck, you will be able to after the will has been read," Fred was trying to console him.

"We do appreciate you and Julie being here. I don't think Sarah would have coped without someone around her. I didn't think she would ever get over losing her mother."

As they reached the yard, the smell of pasties cooking reached them. Sarah and Julie were sitting on the seat outside the door in the sun. "Smells like you've been busy."

"Oh, not us; it's the Aga," Sarah said with a big smile.

"I won't live that down, will I," Fred replied.

"No," the girls said together.

The rest of the day and evening was spent chatting and speculating about the reading of the will. George was over in the barn with the owl. Every whip and while Fred would go out and spend some time with him. The last time he went out, he returned to get the others. "Come on over to the barn, quietly," he said.

They all followed; they tiptoed up the steps, and there was George, sitting on a five gallon can and the owl sitting on his knee. "Shh," Sarah whispered, "let's leave him." They started to walk out. George turned and saw them; his face just glistened.

Sarah crept over quietly and kissed him on the cheek. The owl looked up at her, and I swear it winked its eye at her.

George put his hand out and the owl went onto his hand. He stood up and put his hand up to the beam and the owl flew onto it. He went out and followed the others back to the house. They all had a drink and went to bed.

The next morning, they all sat down to breakfast. "What are you going to do today?" Sarah asked John. "You have to do something to occupy your mind. It will seem a long day waiting for tonight."

"I think I'll get Fred and George to help me clean out

that old shed out up the top of long acre. It will be handy to put the cows and calves in, in winter."

"You can't do that," Julie blurted out.

"Pardon," John said. He was so surprised, he didn't quite know what to say.

"I mean ..." Julie started to reply, and then there was a long pause.

"Yes, what do you mean?" Sarah asked, with a big grin on her face.

Julie was getting embarrassed. Her face went deep red. "I just meant it's not winter yet." Julie was trying to get out of a difficult situation.

"You sure that shed doesn't mean something special to you?" Sarah was making fun of her now. "What about you, Fred?" she asked, thinking she would embarrass him, as well. "Do you think John should clean the shed out?"

But Fred, ever the diplomat, had the answer. "Yes, I think he should clear the shed out, but not now. There's some good hay in there, and it might be handy to keep it up there. If you get short of grass, you could feed it to the stock that's up there."

Julie butted in. "That's what I meant," her face turning back to normal.

But it was not to last, as Sarah said, "Really? How do you know there's hay in there?"

"I just do. Now I must go and make my bed." And she walked out of the kitchen.

Sarah went over and whispered in John's ear, "leave the shed. I think it's a love nest." John smiled and patted her on the bum.

Julie returned to the kitchen. As she came in, John said, "I think we'll leave the shed. That was a good idea of yours, Fred. I think our time would be better spent making sure the silos are all ready for when we start the harvest."

The three men went out. Sarah and Julie were left in the kitchen. "You bugger," Julie said, "you're a proper bugger."

"Whatever do you mean?" Sarah was smiling as she replied.

"You know what I mean. Now let's change the subject." Julie had heard quite enough about the shed.

She had done the dishes and sat down at the table; Sarah was beginning to get upset again. "I do hope things will be sorted out tonight. I do so want to bury my baby," she said with tears in her eyes. "I thought a lot of lord Trelivan, but it doesn't seem right that I can't make funeral arrangements until his are sorted out."

"My dear Sarah, I know how you must feel. But with a bit of luck, you might be able to tomorrow." Julie did feel for her.

"I know when Mum died there was lots to do. Miss Pollard was marvelous; she made most of the arrangements, and I had no money to pay the undertaker. Lord Trelivan paid the bill. He was good to all his tenants." Sarah was feeling better thinking of all the good Lord Trelivan had done. "Julie, dear, I do want to talk about it. I think it helps." Sarah had a hundred things on her mind. "I was thinking of bearers," she continued. "I think we only need one. Do you think Fred would carry her?"

"Oh, I'm sure he would consider it an honour, but are you sure John doesn't want to?" Julie said. "You should discuss it with him first."

"I know I should, but I find it so hard to talk to him. I feel so guilty that I lost his baby." Sarah was now getting really upset.

"You did not lose his baby, and you need to get those thoughts out of your head right now. Only one person is to blame, and we all know who that is, don't we." Julie was getting angry. "Now come on, dry your eyes. We'll go for a little walk before we get dinner."

"Where, up to the shed?" There was a smile back on Sarah's face.

"No," Julie replied abruptly, "we will go up to the field with the wildflowers. I like it up there."

Sarah blew her nose and wiped her eyes again. "I know," she said, "I've got the potatoes and an onion peeled. If you get the chops, we can put them in a casserole dish and it can cook slowly whilst we're gone."

"Good idea," Julie replied as she went to the fridge and got the chops out. She handed them to Sarah.

"I thought you got five chops," Sarah said, as she laid them in the dish.

"Yes, I did," Julie replied.

"Well, there's only four here," she said.

"I'm sure there were five, as I watched the butcher cut them. Perhaps he left one on his block, but I think I would have noticed." Julie felt she should have paid a bit more attention to the butcher.

"Never mind, they are quite big. There's plenty here," Sarah said as she popped them into the oven.

"We better just tell the boys we're off," Sarah said, as they walked across the yard. "We're going for a walk," she shouted, "and don't worry about dinner. The Aga's doing it."

They walked up across the fields until they came to the meadow. The sun was shining, which was making the grass glisten between the flowers. Julie looked at Sarah. "Isn't this beautiful," she said, "isn't nature marvelous? No human could create this. I hope it stays like this forever."

"You are quite the romantic, aren't you?" Sarah said as they walked through the meadow. They reached the mill pond and sat on the grass.

"This is the best place in the world," Julie said as she lay back and looked at the sky.

"Oh, I thought the shed was," Sarah was teasing again.

"I've heard more than enough about the shed for one day, thank you." Julie was enjoying the joke quietly. "Shall we stay here a while?" she said.

They were there for quite a while; Julie looked up and noticed Sarah was crying. "What is it?" she said, as she put her arm around her.

"I was just thinking what a wonderful place this would be to bring a baby. Can you just imagine a little girl playing in the flowers? Making posies, putting them in their hair, bringing a bunch home for her mum. My little girl won't. My little girl is dead."

Julie didn't know what to say. Her eyes just filled with tears and they cried together. After a few minutes, Sarah took a hanky out of her pocket and dried her eyes. "Come on," she said, "we better go back, as the Aga won't cook the veg unless we put it on."

"I know you're upset, but if it's any consolation, I know you would have made a good mother, and you will one day. You mark my words," Julie said, as they made their way back to the yard.

They got back to the yard. "Dinner in half an hour," Sarah shouted. "That's if the Aga has done its job." They went on in. It wasn't long before the men followed.

"A funny thing this morning," Julie said. "I'm sure I got five chops yesterday, but this morning there were only four. And yesterday Sarah thought she had some pasty meat in the fridge, but when she went to get it, it was gone."

George started to walk out of the kitchen, beaming all over his face.

"I think I can solve the mystery," Fred said, looking at George.

George turned and nodded.

"Now we know how the owl is so tame, don't we, George,"

Fred said, with as big a smile as George. He put his hand on his shoulders. "We can go down the butcher's this afternoon and get some more."

They had their dinner. Fred and George had gone down to the butcher's and came back with enough meat to last the owl for a week.

It was now approaching the time to go for the will reading. "We'll look after George whilst you're gone," Julie said.

"No, we are going to take George with us, and we want you two there as moral support, don't we, dear," John said as he looked at Sarah.

"Yes, it's the first time I've faced anyone since I lost the baby, and I do need you two there," Sarah said, holding back the tears again.

They got down to the pub. Inside was done out with the tables in rows with a small stage in front. The two solicitors were there showing people to their seats. They led them up to the front tables. They were soon joined by Cart the blacksmith. Miss Pollard was on one of the three seats on the stage. The whole village had turned out. Rupert Trelivan came in. He was dressed in a tweed jacket plus four trousers and a deerstalker hat. He had never dressed like that before; he was certainly playing the part of the squire. He picked up a chair and put it on the stage beside the two empty ones that were for the solicitors.

They came up on the stage, and Miss Pollard introduced them.

"Good evening, ladies and gentlemen," Mr Knight said. He then went on to explain. "This is quite unusual to have a will read in this way. In fact, this is an unusual will, and it'll have quite an effect on a few people's lives. As you see, we have the lovely Miss Pollard with us. She is here to help us with something, if she is needed. Now, without more ado, I'll pass you over to Mr Starkey to read the will."

— 59 —

Mr Knight sat down and Mr Starkey stood up. "Good evening, ladies and gentlemen, without further ado. This is the last will and testament of Lord Charles Richard Edward Trelivan, and this is a short statement in his words.

"This estate was bought by my great-grandfather and continued to be built up by my Grandfather and father. Their motto was to look after their workers and tenants and they will look after them. And I hope I have continued in the same vein.

"Now, for the will," Mr Starkey continued.

"To all the estate workers, with the exception of Miss Pollard, who we will get to later, I leave one hundred pounds each. To my great friend who has come up and sat with me on many occasions, (he's a giant of a man with a soft heart, we all know him as Cart but I have to legally use his real name), so, to Jim Bird I leave him his blacksmith's shop cottage an one thousand pounds.

"To Ben Write, the landlord of The Butcher's Arms, I leave him the pub, providing he remains the landlord for ten years. I have done this as I know the part he plays in the heart of the village." Mr Starkey paused and took a drink of water, and then he continued with Lord Trelivan's words.

"Tremarrow Farm, all its land and cottages, with the exception of Rose Cottage, also approximately two hundred and fifty acres and buildings known as Stony Moor mine fields, I leave to my daughter and son-in-law Mr and Mrs J. Brite."

The whole room was filled with people muttering. Rupert Trelivan jumped up. "This can't be right!" he shouted. "Let me see. You are making it up," he continued.

Mr Knight got up. "Will you please sit down or leave the room," he said firmly.

Rupert pointed to Sarah. "You haven't heard the last of this," he shouted as he sat down. Sarah was crying. Mr Starkey looked down at her. "I know it's confusing and upsetting dear, but I do have to continue."

He had another drink of water, then continued. "Rose Cottage and two thousand pounds I leave to my good companion, Miss Olive Pollard.

"The manor house, the farms and cottages, in fact all the rest of the estate, I leave to the National Trust.

"All money and securities left after all debts are paid, I leave to my daughter Sarah, as I know she will use some of it to benefit my son, George Page."

The whole room was full of chatter again.

Rupert jumped up again. "This can't be right! What have I got?"

"Nothing," Mr Knight replied. "Absolutely nothing." He had a look of contentment on his face.

"They can't be his children. I'm his only child. I will contest the will. I know much cleverer solicitors than you pair of prats," he continued.

Mr Knight turned to him. "It doesn't matter how clever your solicitors are. There is nothing they can do," he said. "You see, Rupert, Lord Trelivan is not your father."

The whole room gasped. "That's why Miss Pollard is here. She will explain all."

Miss Pollard rose to her feet. She was looking very flummoxed. "Now, my dears, let me see. I can only tell it as it is. Lord Trelivan went to South America just after he got married. He went to help his cousin. His cousin owned a mine, and there had been a terrible accident with much loss of life. His cousin was devastated. He was at the point of suicide when he got out there. Anyway he was away for three years." She turned towards Rupert, "And you were born at the end of the second."

"You're lying," Rupert shouted, "you're lying! I would have known, someone would have said, and how would you know."

"Let me see how would I know? Well, my dear, you see, when your mother knew she was pregnant she confided in me. She wrote to Lord Trelivan. He loved her dearly, and he forgave her without even seeing her. He wrote back to both of us, asking if I could help. I was only seventeen and had just come through a terrible ordeal. I had decided to stay with my older sister who had moved to Somerset to live." Miss Pollard took a long drink of water. You could tell she was somewhat emotional. "Anyway, it was decided that your mother would come with me to Somerset until the baby was born. We would pretend that we had been out to see Lord Trelivan. If we stayed away until you were about a year old, no one would realise the dates. We stayed with my sister until Lord Trelivan returned, and we all came back together. No one ever knew he was not your father."

"How do I know if this is true? This is a plot to stop me having what's mine. You're all in it together!" Rupert was going wild. "How can that thing down there be my father's son?" he was pointing to George.

Cart the blacksmith got to his feet and walked up to George and put his arm around him. "This man here with all his disabilities is far more of a man than you will ever be," he said, pointing to Rupert. "You make me ashamed to say this, but I feel I have to. If you want the whole truth, I'm …" (the whole room went so quiet, wondering what was coming, you could hear a pin drop.) "I'm your uncle; my brother was your father. But I'm afraid to say I have no feelings for you whatsoever. I don't consider you as any part of my family, and I never will."

Mr Starkey tried to get some calm. "That's it, ladies and gentleman. If you could all leave us now, except for John and Sarah."

Sarah was still sitting down, feeling completely bemused. "Is this all true? I'm … I'm in a dream," she said. "Why, oh why didn't he tell me? Why didn't my mum?"

Mr Knight got down from the stage and sat down beside Sarah. "If it is any consolation," he said, "I have known your father for many years. He yearned to tell you, but he wouldn't tell out of respect for your mother. What he never realised was that your mother wanted it kept quiet not to protect her, but to protect him. If only I could have convinced him of this, things would have been so different." He passed Sarah a letter. "He asked me to give you this."

Mr Knight put his arm around Sarah. He seemed such a caring man. "Now, my dear, I'm afraid we have to talk about the arrangements. The reason we brought all this out in the open before the funeral was due to your sad loss. We wondered that once you knew who your father was, you might want your baby buried with her grandfather."

Sarah was wiping the tears from her eyes. "I don't know what to say. I feel numb. I don't want to open this letter now. My stomach is churning, my heart's thumping, I feel sick." She stood up and caught hold John's hand. "Will you take me home now," she said. She turned to Mr Knight. "I'm sorry, but I don't know what to say. Can I see you tomorrow? You have been so kind."

"Of course, my dear, you go home and sleep on it. Think hard about the decision you make, discuss it with John and try not to do anything you might regret later on. We can't leave it too long before we make arrangements, but I would sooner take a day longer than make the wrong decision."

His words were comforting to Sarah. She looked up and gave him a kiss on the cheek as they left.

No one spoke as they walked home. So much had happened; there was a lot of excitement and sorrow, yet no one knew what to say.

When they got back, they went into the kitchen. Sarah flopped down in the armchair, clutching her letter. Julie put the kettle on. Still no one spoke. Sarah looked as if she was in another world.

Fred broke the silence. "Would you like us to go and give you and John some privacy?"

"No, no," Sarah replied, "I want you all here. I need you all." She turned to Julie. "Will you read my letter to me?"

"Oh, Sarah dear, of course I will. But I don't think it's right; it's personal to you." Julie was afraid what it might contain.

"I can't read it, I can't read it. But I want to know what is in it. Somebody help me, please." Sarah was getting very upset.

"Come on, love, don't upset yourself," John said as he knelt down beside the chair and put his arm around her. He took the letter out of her hand and gave it to Julie. "Go on, read it," he whispered.

Julie opened the letter. Her hands were shaking. Her eyes were filling up with tears. Fred realised she would not be able to read it. "Here, let me," he said as he took the letter out of her hand. "Of course, if that's alright with you, Sarah."

Sarah nodded in approval.

Fred sat on the chair at the end of the table. He lay the letter on the table and began to read it.

*My Darling Sarah,*

*I hope you can forgive me and your mother for this. I know it must be very difficult for you. I loved your mother dearly, and her me. Had things been different, I would have asked her to marry me. But I was still married to a lady that I also loved, and still do to this day. Her disappearance was a mystery, and it still is.*

*Your mother was such a comfort to me when my wife disappeared that we got closer and closer. We didn't plan to fall in love. It just happened. And it was love; real love.*

*I hope you won't think of me as a cad for loving two people. I wanted everyone to know that I was your father, but your mother didn't. God knows how hard it was for me. But I promised your mother I would keep it a secret until I died.*

*I don't know if you can remember anything of when you were small – how I used to nurse you and George, the games we played, the fun we had – just like a normal family.*

*When you started school, your mother insisted that you not come up to the manor as much, as people would get suspicious. I told her it didn't matter. I said, let's tell the world.*

*Your mother insisted we tell no one. Her words still remain with me. She said, 'We have two beautiful children, born out of love, not lust, and it must remain our secret always."*

*I reluctantly obeyed her wish.*

*I did consider leaving you the whole of the estate, but I don't think it would bring you happiness, and that's why I have done what I have.*

*Once again, I hope you can forgive me. I wish you, George and John love, health and happiness in the future.*

*Good night, God bless, my darling daughter.*
*Love, Dad*

"Oh God," Sarah said, "what a pair of bloody fools they were. Why, oh why didn't they tell me. I don't know if I can forgive them."

John caught hold of her hand. "We have to decide what we are going to do about the funeral."

"I know, but I don't know what to say. How can we make a decision? We don't know what he would have wanted. Please, John, you say what you think." Sarah was making a plea for help.

"I know your mother loved you immensely, and from what I know of our visits to Lord Trelivan, although I didn't realise it at the time, the way he used to hold your hand, the way he used to smile when you walked in, how he always sat beside you when we stayed for tea, how he always kissed your cheek when we left. He never did any of those things to anyone else." John continued, "The more I think of it now, the more I think we should have realised there was more to it than just friendship. And if you remember when we got married, why did he let us rent the farm? And the money he gave us. I think we were very naive not to realise then how special you were to him."

Sarah's eyes were bulging where she had been wiping the tears. "I would give all this up," she said, "if I could have just known when I was growing up. I do believe he loved me; if only he had told me. What shall we do about our baby? You decide, dear. Your mind is clearer than mine." Sarah was hoping John would make the decision.

"It's not a decision for me to make alone. It has to be what we both want, and I don't think we should make a decision until we have slept on it." John felt it too much responsibility to have on his shoulders. "Let's all have a cup of tea and get to bed. With a bit of luck, things might look clearer in the morning."

The next morning, whilst they were all sitting down having breakfast, there was knock at the door.

"I can't believe the solicitors are here already." Sarah was getting flummoxed. "Keep them talking for a minute," she said, picking up the dishes as fast as she could.

Julie went out and answered the door. It was Cart the blacksmith. He was dressed in brown corduroys, a white short-sleeve shirt, with green check. He had a vest with sleeves that came below the shirt sleeves, a waist coat with a pocket watch in one of the pockets and a chain attached to the other side. He also had a peak cap which he removed when Julie opened the door. "Miss Sarah around?" he asked.

"Come on in," Sarah shouted, hearing his voice. "To

what do we owe this pleasure?"

"Guilt, I suppose," Cart replied. "The fact that I have kept quiet about Rupert all these years. I should have stopped the misery he caused years ago. I never told out of respect for your father, as he had accepted him as his son. The problem was, right up to his death, he thought his wife might return, and that's why he wouldn't disown him. God knows what happened to her. She knew how much your father loved her. She could not take the abuse she received from Rupert anymore; well, that's my take on it, anyway."

"Did you know he was my father?" Sarah asked.

"No, dear, I had no idea. I did ask you mother once. She more or less told me to mind my own business. It's for me to know and you never to find out she said. I never asked her again; it was none of my business."

Sarah put a cup of tea down in front of him. They all sat around the table listening to what he had to say. All except George, that is; no one had noticed he had got a tin of spam out of the cupboard and was over by the sink opening it. Once he had opened the tin, he put the meat in his pocket. "Owl," he said, walking to the door, as if to let everyone know where he was going.

Cart started again, "Back to what I was saying. I didn't know he was your father, but the more I think back I should have realised. I don't know how much you can remember of when you were small, but I have great memories. I had to put a swing up for George on the old beech tree in the middle of the great lawn. Then one on a branch on the other side for you when you came along. I remember one sunny autumn afternoon, there was a strong breeze blowing. I had just finished putting some railings up around the pond to stop you from falling in. It was rather hot and I sat at the top of the big lawn. Looking down to the big tree, I could see you on one swing and your mother on the other. Your father was pushing you, then running around the tree to push your mother. The leaves were falling in abundance, some on you. Every time your father ran in front of you, laughter just filled the air. I remember thinking, I wish I knew love like that. There were a number of occasions like that. But it still never crossed my mind that he was your father."

"I do remember the swing. I can remember falling down and grazing my knee. Lord Trelivan kissed it better." Sarah was feeling more relaxed about the situation. "I remember we used to go there every day. I can remember staying some nights. I slept in a big four poster bed with George. I think I used to think they were relations, but I don't remember Rupert being there."

Cart continued to explain. "When you were born, the war was on. Rupert was called up for national service. He wrangled his way out of it somehow. He had a job in the war office in London. He stayed in London for a while after the war. You must have been eight or nine when he came back. Now I think back, that's when you and your mum stopped coming up to the big house as much. You should ask Miss Pollard. She knows more than me."

With that there was another knock on the door. This time it was the solicitors. "Look, I must be off," Cart said, getting up from the chair. "If there is anything I can do, you know where to find me."

"Thanks. You don't realise how much you've done already," Sarah said as she reached up and kissed his cheek.

Mr Knight and Mr Starkey came into the kitchen. "Sit down," John said, pointing to the chair.

"Julie and I will go for a walk and leave you to it," Fred said.

"You don't have to," Sarah replied.

"Yes, I think it's best. You must have a bit of privacy. Come on, Julie, put your shoes on. We will check on George." On the way, Fred and Julie made their way to the barn to check on George. He was sitting down in the barn with the owl on one knee and a big lump of spam on the other. The owl kept pecking at it.

"You coming with us?" Julie asked, hoping for a no. She wanted Fred to herself. She knew Fred would have asked if he wanted to come. She thought if she asked it would please Fred.

George shook his head. "Owl," he said.

"See you later, George," they both said as they walked out of the barn.

"Come on," Julie shouted, running up across the field beside the yard.

"Where are we going?" Fred shouted.

"Up to the field with the wild flowers, and then if you are really good I might let you take me to our shed." She was talking like an excited school girl.

When they got to the meadow, Julie acted like a child running through the flowers, hopping, skipping and jumping, letting her hands flow through the flowers. "Come on," she said, "let's go up the top and we can roll all the way to the bottom."

Fred could see how excited she was, and some of it was rubbing off on him. They got to the top and rolled all the way to the bottom, ending up right on the edge of the mill pond. They both lay back, looking up at the sky. "I want to come up here one night when the stars are shining and make love in the moonlight," Julie said as she put her arms around Fred and cuddled him in.

"When I'm with you like this, my whole body tingles, I get butterflies in my stomach, my head spins. Do you think it will always feel like this?" Sarah was looking down into Fred's eyes as she spoke. "Can we stay here all day?" she asked.

"Of course we can, but I thought you wanted to go to

our shed?" Fred replied, teasing her.

"Oh, yes, I will if that's what you want. I'm sorry." Julie was feeling as if she was leading Fred on.

"Sorry? What are you sorry about?" he asked, stroking her hair.

"Sorry that you think I'm leading you on. I did want to go to the shed and make love when we left the farm, but when I got here, this place is so magical I just want to stay here and hold you. Come on, let's go to the shed," she said, standing up and reaching down to pull Fred up.

They both stood up. Their eyes met and they kissed passionately. Fred gently pushed her back. "You are a silly sausage," he said. "Yes, I enjoy making love to you, but don't you see, there is more to it than that. I love it here, I love just being with you. I could not be more contented than when I have you in my arms. I will never pressure you to make love. It is something that happens when it's right for us both." He gently kissed her.

"I think it's right for us both now," she said as she pulled him to the ground.

Back at the house, Sarah and John were with the solicitors. "Have you made up your mind about the funeral?" Mr Knight asked.

"I have," Sarah said, "but it also depends on John. His dad is buried there as well. I know there's no room by my mum. But John might want her buried with his dad."

"Oh no, Sarah dear, if you want her buried with your dad, that's fine with me. I only suggested it so you had other options and didn't do anything rash."

"I know some of these questions are awkward and upsetting, but the sooner we get the arrangements over with, the easier it will become. I'll tell you what we have arranged, and if you want to alter it, you tell me," Mr Knight said as he opened up a large book. "Now then, the funeral will take place at twelve thirty on July the twelfth at St Mary's church. Afterwards at The Butcher's Arms where the landlord will put on a bit of a do. The bearers for Lord Trlivan will be Cart the blacksmith, Ben the landlord, Albert Rowe the head gardener and Sid Jones from Glebe farm. What about your little girl? Do want to carry her John?"

"I don't think I could," he replied. "We would like our great friend Fred to carry her."

"That's fine. Now don't you worry about a thing. We will sort out everything. Is there anything else you want to ask?

"I don't think so" Sarah replied you are so kind taking care of everything for us.

Then, we must go; we have an appointment with the undertaker. So we'll say goodbye. Here is my card with the office number, and I have written my home number on the back. So if you need me for anything, just call me," Mr Knight said as he handed her the card.

"Let's go and get George and walk up and meet Fred and Julie," John said, putting on his shoes.

"Do you know which way they went?" Sarah asked.

"I'm pretty sure they would have gone up to the mill pond meadow," he replied.

They walked up across the fields. George was chasing a Red Admiral butterfly. It would pitch on some clover, and as soon as George got there, it would fly to the next one. They went through the gate into the meadow. There was no sign of Julie and Fred. They carried on across the meadow. George was still chasing the butterfly.

Suddenly John stopped. He pulled George back by the arm. "Shh," he went, "look over there." They were both lying naked. They where fast asleep in each other's arms. "I think we better go back," John said with a smile on his face.

"I think it's beautiful," Sarah said. "They're so much in love."

They turned and made their way back to the farm. The

butterfly George had chased all the way up he now chased all the way back.

They had been back about an hour, sitting down outside with a cup of tea, when Fred and Julie appeared.

"Where you two been, then?" Sarah asked.

"Just been up to the meadow with the flowers," Julie replied.

"Oh, really? We went up there and didn't see you." Sarah's voice kind of gave it away.

Julie went bright red. "We must have been hidden by the flowers," she replied.

"I don't think the flowers hide much." Sarah was really teasing now.

With that, Miss Pollard came into the yard on her bike. "Hello, dears," she shouted.

"Come on over and sit down," Sarah called as she turned to Julie with a big smile. "Saved by Miss Pollard, I think."

Julie just smiled back. She did wonder if they were seen or not.

"I thought I would just come over and make sure your all right after all the excitement yesterday, and offer my services if you need them."

"Thanks, but I think everything's taken care of. The best thing you can do for me is tell me all about my mum and Lord Trelivan, or Dad, as I call him now." There was so much more Sarah wanted to know. "Have you always known?"

"Yes, dear. Don't think badly of me, but I promised your mum I would never tell."

"Did anyone else know?"

"I think Rupert knew. That's why he was always awful to you; he was so jealous."

"Why? I was no threat to him. Did he know Lord Trelivan wasn't his father?"

"Oh no, dear, he had no idea until the will was read. That

gave me great pleasure."

"Tell me some more about my mum and dad. Cart said they were in love."

The others left and went into the kitchen, leaving Miss Pollard and Sarah sitting on the bench.

Miss Pollard continued. "Yes, dear, they were deeply in love. But the silly fool had to do everything right. He wouldn't let anyone know. He always thought his wife would come back. His love for your mother was far stronger than it was for her. He felt guilty about his wife. He thought he should have done more to protect her."

"What do you mean protect her?"

"Protect her from Rupert. He was horrible and violent to her, although she would never admit it. I saw her legs burnt with a poker, her arms red where he had twisted them. Once I saw her washing and her back was just covered in bruises. Every time anyone asked her what had happened, she made some excuse, like a fall or a horse kicked her. Of course, no one ever believed her. Then one day she just left. No one saw her go or knew where she went, and no one has heard from her to this day."

"Tell me more about when we went up to the big house." Sarah was really excited.

"I don't really know what to tell you. I know the place was full of love when you were all there. It was as if your mother belonged there. It's funny, really. For a house that size, very few people worked there. There was a cook, two maids, your mum and me, and I don't really know what my job was. I think I was part of the fittings. George and you spent most of the summer out on the big lawn playing and having picnics. Your mother and Lord Trelivan were never far behind, you were never out of their sight. They loved the both of you dearly. I do remember one Christmas, we were all sitting around the log fire; all, that is, except for his Lordship. Suddenly Father Christmas appeared in the room. You started to cry because his Lordship wasn't there to see him. Of course, he was Father Christmas. Now, come on, dear, I could murder a cup of tea."

"Oh, of course, come on into the kitchen. What must you think of me." They got up and went indoors. Julie had the kettle on.

They chatted away with Miss Pollard, telling stories about the big house. No one noticed the time.

It wasn't until Julie noticed George going through the cupboards trying to find something to eat. She nudged Sarah as she realized they hadn't yet eaten. "Look," she said, pointing to George.

"Oh, my God, we haven't had any dinner, and now it's tea time."

"That's my fault," Miss Pollard said. "I do go on a bit."

"Not at all," Sarah replied, "it's been wonderful listening to you. Please stay for tea. I don't know what we are going to have."

"Oh no, dear, I must go. I've got a date, you see." Miss Pollard was sounding excited.

"A date?" Sarah said, surprised.

"Oh yes, dear, Cart has asked me over for tea. Hark, and me at my age acting like a school girl. I've never been on a date before." She got on her bike and sped out of the yard.

"Whatever are we going to have for tea, Julie?" Sarah asked.

"I'll go in to Tavy and get fish and chips, if you like," Fred shouted.

"That man is a saint. You're a very lucky girl, you know."

"I sure am," Julie replied.

Fred went off and got the chips. When he got back, they sat around the kitchen table eating them out of the paper.

They were all chatting away about how lovely the place

was. Julie, without thinking about the morning, suddenly said, "My favorite place is the meadow by the pond." She started to blush as she said it.

"I do believe you are blushing," Sarah exclaimed.

John came in on the conversation. "You know, we have called our baby after you; well, I'm going to call that meadow after both of you. From now on it will be known as Julie's Meadow. And it will stay like it is forever. Only good things will ever happen there."

Sarah got up. She had tears in her eyes. She went over and put her arms around him. "You are a big romantic at heart, and I love you to bits," she said as she bent forward and kissed him on the head.

After tea, George went over to see the owl. "Do you mind if I go over with George?" Fred asked politely. He wanted to spend some time with him as he was sure he could get him to talk.

John had gone into the front room to do the farm books. It seemed that was all the room was used for; most of their time was spent in the kitchen. Sarah and Julie stayed sat at the table.

"Are you sure you didn't see us today? Only …"

"Only what, Julie?" Sarah asked.

"Nothing, but I thought, well, you know, the things you said when we got back."

"Oh, those things." Sarah had a big smile on her face, "Now let me see. We saw lots of beautiful things. There was butterfly that seemed to be teasing George; there was the robin that follows me everywhere; there were the flowers in the meadow; oh, and let me think, I'm sure there was something else. It might come to me in a minute."

"Come on, you're just teasing me. Did you or didn't you see us?"

"What was there to see? Would it make you embarrassed?"

"I don't know, really. If you love someone, some things should be private. But if you love someone as much as I love Fred, then the whole world should know. I would hate to think someone saw us making love, though. Julie was getting quite emotional."

Sarah decided to end the game. "Yes, we did see you. All we could see were your heads. We thought you were asleep; we didn't want to wake you, so we came back to the farm."

"Thank goodness for that. We were naked, you know," Julie whispered.

"Perhaps we should have had a closer look, then." Sarah was smiling; she knew how beautiful they looked.

"Do you believe in God, go to church and all that?"

"My goodness, Julie, whatever brought this on?"

"I didn't. Believe, that is. But don't laugh at me; I'm sure he is up in that meadow. I do believe he is watching over us. Please don't get upset or cross with me, but you know that robin? I think it's you're little baby, I think she will always be here."

"Julie, dear, how could I get upset? I think that's beautiful." Sarah was wiping a tear from her eyes. "I did stop believing, but I'm afraid not to believe. There are too many unanswered questions. Why did he take my mum? Why did he take my baby?"

"I don't think God took your mum or your baby. It was some mad driver that killed your mum, and that bloody Rupert killed your baby. I think God will punish them in some way. When they die, they will never come back. But your mum and baby, they are here with us and they always will be. Hence the robin."

"Julie, Julie, Julie. Wherever did all that come from? I can't believe that came out of your mouth."

"Perhaps God gave the words to me. Perhaps he is trying

to help you come to terms with it through me. I would like to think that's what it is."

"My dear Julie, so would I. Do you really think that's what it is? I would truly like it to be; truly, I would."

There was suddenly an abrupt end as John came back in to the room. "Am I interrupting anything?" He said.

"No, nothing at all," Sarah replied. "Come on, let's go and see the owl."

The door was open when they got to the top of the steps. As they walked in, George was sitting on a can with the owl sitting on his knee, and Fred was trying to teach him words. Sarah caught hold of Julie's hand and squeezed it tight. She looked at the owl. "Mum," she whispered. Sarah squeezed her hand back.

The next few days were much the same. Fred would help John around the farm. Sarah and Julie would spend a lot of time nattering. Fred spent a lot of time with George. Julie and Fred always found a bit of time to go to the meadow.

It was the Sunday before the funeral. They were all sitting down having breakfast. Sarah turned to Julie. "Will you go to church with me this morning?" she asked.

"If you want me to." Julie sounded a little surprised. "What's brought this on?"

"Just been thinking about the things you said."

"What about dinner?" John obviously had other things on his mind.

"We can have roast for tea. You'll enjoy it better the longer you wait. Oh, unless Fred asks the Aga to cook it," Sarah shouted as she went up stairs to change.

After the church service, the vicar asked Sarah if she would stay behind for a minute. They sat on the pew and waited for him to come back in after he had said goodbye to his parishioners.

He came back in and sat down on the pew beside them.

"It's nice to see you here; I hope it helps with your grief."

"Julie helps with my grief," Sarah replied quite bluntly.

"It's good to have friends around you in times like this." The vicar continued, "Now, my dear, I was going to come around and see you this afternoon to ask what hymns you wanted at the funeral, and if anyone wanted to say a few words."

"There is one hymn in particular, "All Creatures Great and Small", and I would like Julie to say a few words."

Julie looked surprised. "I can't say anything. What can I say?"

Sarah just looked at her, full of emotion. "Just tell everyone what you told me," she said.

"You just write a few things down, and I'll have a look at them." The vicar was beginning to wonder what he had let himself in for.

"Oh, I can't write anything; it just comes out. I don't know what's coming."

"On your head be it, then. I'll bid you good morning." The vicar got up and made his way to the vestry.

On the walk back to the farm, the pair were having a bit of a giggle. "I don't think he went much on that, do you?" Julie said.

"They say he can get a bit grumpy sometimes, but I think he will be pleased with what you say. But don't mention anything about being naked." Sarah was smiling as she said it.

Julie gave her a little push like kids having fun.

The days soon passed to the day of the funeral. It was a rather emotional morning. The hearse arrived with baby Julie. It was so sad to see Sarah and John; one would cry, then the other. They tried to comfort each other. Fred spent the morning with George, trying to keep him away from the sorrow. But he knew what was going on. He occasionally wiped a tear from his eye. Fred had got him to speak a sentence; he was hoping that after the funeral he would say it to Sarah.

The time had come to make their way to the church. A large black Bentley pulled up behind the hearse. Sarah, John and George got in. Julie lent forward and gave Sarah a kiss on the cheek. "We'll see you there," she whispered.

"No, wait; there is room in the car for both of you, and I want you with us," Sarah said. "Oh, no," Julie replied, "it wouldn't be right."

"It's right if I say so. Now please get in. I do so much want you with us."

Fred could tell Sarah was getting really upset. He nodded to Julie. "Go on, we better get in." Julie reluctantly obeyed.

The hearse made its way the short journey to the church with precision. At the little crossroads just up from the farm, it meet the hearse carrying Lord Trelivan. It pulled gently out in front of them, and they followed it down to the church.

The service started with the vicar saying a few words, followed by the hymn "All Things Bright and Beautiful". The church was completely full; people were standing right out to the porch. The vicar reluctantly announced that Sarah's friend Julie would like to say a few words.

Both John and Fred gasped. They hadn't been told about this. "Whatever was she going to say?" they both thought. She made her way to the front of the church and stood just in front of the pulpit. She cleared her throat. It was like something stirred from inside as she started to talk.

"This church is certainly a beautiful place.

"My church is a beautiful place, too.

"I talk to God in my church. I don't know if he hears me every time.

"Because I don't believe he can be everywhere at once.

"You see, I like to think that if he's not with me, he's helping someone else.

"Sarah asked me why God chose to take her mother and baby; I don't believe God chose them.

"I think they were unlucky. God was helping someone else at the time, so he couldn't save them.

"As we ask God for forgiveness, he also asks us for forgiveness for not being there when we needed him.

"I believe he returns our loved ones too us, whether it be as a bird, a rabbit or what about that friendly cat that cuddles up on your lap.

"I know we are taught about heaven and hell.

"But who's to say where heaven is?

"I would like to tell you about my church.

"My church has no hymn books, bible or sermons.

"It has things more valuable than gold or silver.

"It has birds that sing, butterflies that flutter around, rabbits that hop and play.

"Grass shimmers in the wind, the vibrant colours of the flowers are like a rainbow on the ground.

"In the wind, the leaves on the big chestnut tree chatter like voices from afar, and the peaceful sound of water flowing in the stream puts your mind completely at rest.

"A place so full of love it makes your body tingle.

"You see, my church is a beautiful meadow. John has named it after their baby; it's called Julie's Meadow. It's the most beautiful place in the world."

She turned to the vicar. "Will you come to my church late tomorrow night and say a prayer for baby Julie?" She turned to the congregation. "I want you all to come at ten o"clock. The moon and stars will be shining then. And everyone bring a candle to light." She suddenly realised what she was saying. She looked down at Sarah, who was drying eyes. "Oh, I'm sorry, Sarah. Will that be all right?"

Sarah broke into a soft smile. "Of course," she said in a very soft voice.

As Julie started to walk to her seat, there was a single clap, then another, then another, then suddenly the whole church clapped.

The vicar had never heard anything like it at a funeral. "Please, please; remember where you are." The place fell silent again.

Julie's mother and father were at the funeral. They could not believe what they had just heard. "Was that really our Julie?" her mother said, nudging her father.

They all slowly followed the coffins to the freshly dug grave. This was probably the most upsetting time for John and Sarah. They were both terribly grief-stricken.

Sarah had her head bowed to the ground. Beside the grave, she suddenly raised her head as she heard, "Chirp, chirp, chirp." There on the gravestone beside her was a robin. Whether it was the one from the farm, who knows, but Sarah believed it was. It brought a gentle smile amongst the tears.

As they turned away from the grave, George was tugging at Sarah's arm.

"Whatever is it, George? What's the matter? Are you all right?"

"Owl," he said, pointing to the large beech tree by the cemetery gate.

There on the lowest branch of the tree was a bright white owl.

Sarah couldn't help herself. "Mum," she shouted.

"Shh," John said as he put her arm around her and led her to the waiting car.

The last thing they wanted to do was go back to The Butcher's Arms, but they thought it their duty to do so.

Julie's mother and father were at the funeral; they also went back to the pub.

"Where did that come from? I would never have believed that was my Julie up there if I hadn't seen it for myself,"

Julie's dad said as he put his arm around her.

"We don't see you much, you know," Julie's mother said, with a touch of disappointment in her voice. "Have you seen anything of Robert since you called off the wedding?"

"No, and I don't want to either. He's the last person I want to see," Julie replied. "Anyway, what did his mother and father say when you told them?"

"They were quite shocked. I think they still think you'll get back together one day."

"What are they, stupid? He makes me feel sick. He's not right. Do they honestly think he could come near me after he's been with a man?"

"Actually, we didn't tell them that bit. We just said you had cold feet. We thought it better that way."

Julie was fuming. "Better; how is it better? Their son's a bloody queer, and I get the blame for calling off the wedding. I'll get Fred to drive me over there and I'll soon tell them about their bloody son."

Julie's father butted in. "Where's that compassionate girl that was speaking in the church?" he said.

"Oh yes, I'm compassionate, all right. But I also know right from wrong, and what he is doing is wrong." Julie was really getting uptight.

Her mother was trying to say all the right things, but just putting her foot in it. "I know you might not think so, but it's probably because you're jealous that you feel the way you do."

"Mother, you do come out with the stupidest of things. Why on earth would I be jealous? If you really want to know, I went to see him to call the wedding off because I didn't love him and I never have. I never realised I was in love with Fred."

"Oh, now the truth is coming out. How long has that been going on? I might have guessed there was more to it.

You're no better than he is."

"You make me mad, Mother. Nothing was going on with me and Fred. Anyway, if there was, it's a bit different than being queer."

"I don't condone what he's doing, and if you were seeing Fred behind his back I wouldn't condone that either."

"I wasn't going out with Fred, I made up my mind to call the wedding off before anything happened between me and Fred, and if you don't believe me, you can't know your own daughter very well."

Her father put his arms around her. "Now, come on, dear," he said, "I would never doubt your integrity. I hope you will be very happy together. I'm afraid you wouldn't like to hear what I think of Robert. I always thought there was something strange about that friend of his, Julian Sleep. Now, come on, my girl, you go over with your friends. Me and your mother will get along home."

She stretched up and gave him a kiss. "Thanks, Dad," she whispered in his ear.

Julie went back over to the corner of the pub where her friends were. The talk was about the absence of Rupert Trelivan. "Do you think that's the last we will see of him?" Fred asked Cart, who was leaning against the wall.

"I'd like to think so. But I can't see him going this quiet. I bet he's got something up his sleeve."

Cart put his arm around Julie. "Come here, my dear," he said, "do you know you made me cry in church? No bugger's done that before. I think the old vicar was lost for words for the first time in his life. People run the younger generation down, but you're a credit to them. In fact, all four of you are."

The five of them said their goodbyes, Sarah and John thanked people for coming, and they made their way home. When they got back to the yard, sitting on the top step of the barn was the owl, and on an old milk churn at the bottom of the steps was the robin.

The next morning at breakfast, Sarah asked Julie if they should make some sausage rolls for the evening.

"I don't know. Do you think anyone will come? I don't really know what we will do up there," she replied.

"Don't tell me that. Now, you must have had some idea at the time."

"Of course, I do. We are all going to light a candle for baby Julie, and we will make sausage rolls even if there's only us five there."

"I've got some sausage meat in the fridge, so we will get on with it right after breakfast." Sarah was sounding quite cheerful under the circumstances.

George suddenly crept out of the room.

Fred tapped Sarah on the shoulder. "I don't go much on your chances of the sausage meat being there," he said.

"George," Sarah shouted. He came back in to the kitchen, very sheepish.

Fred suddenly thought it was time he said his new words. He went over and whispered in his ear.

George's face lit up like a thousand candles. "I love you, Sarah," he said.

Sarah came across the kitchen and put her arms around him. "I love you, too," she said, the tears running down her cheek. "And don't worry about the sausage meat. We can soon nip down the butcher's and get some more."

George nodded in approval. "You two sit down and have a natter, and we'll go down the village and get the meat," John said, putting on his shoes.

"When we get back the Aga can cook the sausage rolls," Fred shouted.

"Let's have another cup of tea," Julie said, putting the kettle on.

"I wonder where Rupert is; I feel a little bit sorry for him." Sarah was sounding a bit concerned.

"Sorry for him? How can you possibly be sorry for him, after what he's done?"

"Well, if he is jealous of me, then perhaps it's my fault he is the way he is."

"How can it be your fault? See what Miss Pollard said he did to his mother – you weren't around then. The man's an absolute bastard."

"Where's the God in you now? Where's the forgiveness?"

"God doesn't forgive everyone; you have to earn it, and even God has to earn it."

"I could not have got through this without you, Julie dear," Sarah said as she reached across the table and caught hold her hands. "I don't mind if it's just the five of us up there tonight, it will mean so much to me. I'm so glad you suggested it. Shall we go up there every night and light a candle?"

Julie squeezed her hand tight. "Oh, I didn't tell you," she said, with a big smile on her face. "God said some nights, Fred and I have to be there on our own."

Sarah replied, "This God seems to be on your side, if you ask me. He's a pretty good mate."

"He sure is," she replied, "he sure is."

That evening they went up to the meadow. Sarah carried a biscuit tin with three dozen sausage rolls in it. It was still daylight when they got there. The owl perched on the bottom branch of the chestnut tree, and the robin was on a large stone beside the mill pond.

"Do you think anyone will come?" Fred said rather anxiously.

"Doesn't matter who comes. All that matters is that we're here together," John replied.

It soon became dark. "No one is coming. Let's have a

sausage roll, and then we can light our candles." Julie was sounding disappointed.

Little did they know that instead of coming through the farmyard and up across the fields, the villagers had come up the lane and crept down across the meadow. They had assembled themselves about twenty yards away without being seen. Suddenly they started to sing. The whole valley was filled with the sound of "All Things Bright And Beautiful'.

"My God," Sarah exclaimed, "look, the entire village has come. They have all come for my baby." She turned to Julie. "We haven't got enough sausage rolls."

"Trust you to think of that. I don't think anyone will worry about that. Just be happy," Julie said.

Miss Pollard appeared from the crowd. "I hope you don't mind, dears, I brought a few sausage rolls along. I thought people might be hungry."

Sarah and Julie looked at each other and smiled. "Thanks a lot," Sarah said.

"Hello, my dear, came a voice." Julie looked around. "Oh, Vicar, it's you!" she exclaimed.

"Yes, you came to my church. I thought it only fair I come to yours. And please call me Andrew."

"Will you say some prayers tonight?" Sarah asked.

"If that's all right with Julie. After all, it is her church."

"Of course, it's all right with me. There is nothing we would like more."

Cart came over and pulled a mouth organ out of his pocket. "Come on, gather around. Let's have a song or two." And everyone formed a semicircle and they all sang and sang. This went on to midnight; one or two gradually dropped out of the singing and sat on the ground. Then a few more and a few more.

It ended up with everyone sitting on the ground, eating a sausage rolls. Julie stood up in front of them. "Now it's time for what we came for. I would like to ask my new friend Andrew to say a prayer. Then anyone who has brought a candle, if they would like to, can light it and place it around the pool."

A prayer was said for baby Julie and everyone placed a lit candle around the pool. There must have been around a hundred candles glowing in the moonlight.

Suddenly, "Look," John shouted. Everyone looked towards the pool, and there in the water was the refection of an angel.

"God, it's a miracle!" Andrew exclaimed.

Everyone who was there saw it. There was absolutely no doubt it was an angel.

"Have you ever seen an angel before, Andrew?" Julie asked.

"No, I have never seen anything like that in my life. We are very privileged for God to choose us to witness such a thing."

"Oh, Andrew, do you think he would choose my church over yours? Why would he do that?"

"God moves in mysterious ways, my child."

"This is where you and I differ. I don't believe he does. I don't believe he chooses us. I believe there are angels everywhere, and tonight we were lucky to see one. Don't you think your religion is confusing?"

"Most things in life are, dear."

"But they could be much simpler. I believe in God; I think it is the same God as yours. But do you honestly think he chooses us? Where do you stop with it? Do you think he chooses who is going to be rich and who is going to be poor? Which football team is going to win? And what about when my nan's cat when it got caught in a rabbit trap. Did he chose that as well? I still think you're either lucky or unlucky. God tries to protect us, but he can't be everywhere at once. But he always tries to make amends when someone slips through."

"So many questions I haven't got answers for. All I know is, as long as you believe, he will always have a special place in his heart for you. As I do, my dear. If ever I had a daughter, I would love for her to be like you." Andrew was filling up with emotion.

The dedication was ended by people drifting away and Sarah coming over and putting her arms around Julie. "This is the best friend anyone could ever have," she said.

"I am quite sure of that," Andrew replied. "I think you are two wonderful people, and with all that's going on in the world today, you are a credit to your generation. In fact you all are, and whether you come to church or not, I hope we can remain friends."

"Always," Julie said, as she leaned up and gave him a kiss on the cheek.

# Chapter 2

Not a lot happened over the next few weeks. Fred said he would stay until the end of the harvest. Julie said she would stay as long as they would have her, even though her mum kept on insisting she get a job.

The harvest was going well. Julie was out in the fields with the men. Sarah would bring out lunch every day, and they would sit and have a picnic. Fred and Julie spent many nights out walking through the meadow. And I'm sure a few evenings were spent in the shed. Fred went in to Tavistock library a few times to try and find out more about George's condition.

It was the last day of the harvest. There was a lorry loading the last load of straw; there were still one or two bales scattered around. Fred was sitting on one of them, looking up towards the lorry. Julie was being chatted up by the driver. She quite enjoyed that. She was wearing the shortest pair of hot pants you ever saw, and she had a blouse with no buttons; it was tied in the front, showing her midriff and deep cleavage.

John came up and sat down beside Fred. "Are you jealous?" he asked.

"Far from it," he said, "far from it. I was just thinking how lucky I am. Have you ever seen anyone more beautiful?"

"Don't let Sarah here me say this, but I have to agree with you. She has to be one of the most beautiful girls in the world. And yes, you are bloody lucky."

"Come on, Fred, let's get back. I think we should all go down the pub tonight for a meal."

"That sounds good to me," Fred replied. Julie walked down and sat down beside them. Fred told her they were going down the pub for a meal.

"Come on, then, let's go and get our glad rags on." Julie was obviously up for it.

"You should wear what you have on; Ben's trade would more than double if people knew you were there," John said with a big smile.

They went back to the farm and got changed and made their way down to the pub. George went up to see the owl before they went. The owl was so tame now that she only had to hear his footsteps and she would fly to meet him.

They sat down at a table in the middle of the pub. Cart and Miss Pollard were sitting at a table beside them. They exchanged pleasantries. It wasn't long before they were engrossed in conversation.

"Have you been to church lately?" Cart asked, looking at Julie.

"Afraid not," she replied.

"Well, you haven't half changed the vicar. His sermons are a lot different now, and I can only put it down to you."

With that, Andrew walked in the door. "Speak of the devil," Cart said with a loud voice.

"I hope you don't mean that literally," Andrew replied.

"Oh, no, you silly bugger. I was just saying I think this girl changed your way of thinking a bit."

"I'm not sure about that. Let's just say she made me think." Andrew turned to John. "I'm glad I've seen you. I keep meaning to come over, but you know how it is, with one thing and another. I wanted to ask you if we could hold harvest festival up in your meadow this year. It was such a good evening last time we were there; I think it would go down very well."

"Of course, you can. We can put a few bales of straw up there for people to sit on and we can make a platform for the produce. The only thing is, there aren't many flowers, as they have all gone to seed." John was sounding quite excited about it.

"That doesn't matter. The setting is still beautiful and now, with the evenings beginning to pull in, we could have a few candles again."

All of a sudden, the door of the pub opened and in walked Rupert Trelivan with a lady of quiet distinction. "Guess who's back. Look, everyone, it's Mother. She's back."

Everyone looked in amazement. Could it really be her? She came over to Cart and Miss Pollard. "Why, Miss Pollard, you have hardly changed a bit. Nor have you, Cart, come to that. I have missed you all. It just feels like I have never been away."

"Sit down here, then, and tell us where you have been," Cart said as he pulled a chair out from under the table.

"Not much to tell. It seems that I have lost my memory for years. I have been living and working in London, for what, let me see, it must be twenty-five years or more. It was just by chance I happened to be working on reception at the old conservative club. Rupert came in to tell some old friends about his father. When he mentioned his name, it was like a jolt to my memory and it all started to come back. The doctors always told me it would happen like that one day."

"Can you remember what a bastard that son of yours was to you?" Cart asked sarcastically.

"Oh, come now. Rupert wasn't a bad boy; not really. You used to exaggerate a bit, didn't you, Miss Pollard?"

"No, I don't think I did. I wouldn't use the language Cart did, but I remember what I saw." Miss Pollard was sounding quite angry.

Rupert came over beside them. "You lot want to watch what you're saying, or you could find yourself homeless," he said. "We have top lawyers in London contesting the will. Everything will soon belong to its rightful owner."

"Now, come, dear, we haven't come back to put people

out of their homes. These good people were all my friends once, and I hope they will be again one day."

Rupert looked at John and Sarah. "That doesn't include you pair," he said.

"Come on, Sarah," John said, "let's go home." All five of them stood up.

"Don't go. Don't let the bastard spoil your evening." Cart shouted over to Ben the landlord, "I thought this bastard was banned."

Ben walked over. "Yes, come on, out you go. The lady can stay, but you're not welcome here."

"Come on, Mother, we know where we are not welcome. You lot will be the losers, just you wait and see. You will all regret this," he shouted as they went out the door.

They all stayed and finished their meal. There was only one topic of conversation throughout: was she really Lady Trelivan? She seemed to know an awful lot about them, and with a pub full of people, she came right over to Cart and Miss Pollard. I don't think there was any doubt in their minds that she was. Even though neither one of them would have recognised her.

With all the talk about what could happen now, no one paid much attention to the time. The next thing, PC Roberts came in the door. "What's going on?" he said. "This isn't like you, Ben, allowing after-hours drinking. Well, not without locking the doors. I hope you got a good explanation, or I shall have to report it."

"Now, you know I wouldn't allow after-hours drinking. I like my bed too much for that. You better sit down and I'll tell you about it." PC Roberts sat on a stool by the bar and listened intensely.

"Bloody hell," he said, you better give me a whiskey.

PC Roberts downed his whiskey in one. "Come on, you lot, if Sergeant Gibbs comes along, we will all be for the high jump. Now, off home you go," he said with authority.

They all left the pub and were laughing and joking as they walked up the road. John said he thought it would be good to have the harvest festival up in the meadow.

"I expect the vicar thinks he might see another miracle. I would love to see another one. It was beautiful," Sarah said excitedly.

"What about you Julie," John asked with a big smile on his face, do you see any miracles up in that shed?"

"Oh, plenty in there," she replied.

Sarah couldn't be left out of the joke. "I suppose you're responsible for them, Fred."

"Don't bring me in to it. I only go up there to check on the hay."

"That's a new name for it: check on the hay." Sarah was quite giggly as she said it.

They got back to the yard and owl was once again sitting on the top step of the barn. George ran up the steps and the owl flew onto his shoulder. The others went on indoors and left him with the owl.

It was the next morning when things started to sink in about the return of Lady Trelivan. As they were having breakfast, Mr Knight arrived on the doorstep. "Good morning, dears. I have just come around, as I believe you all had an encounter in the pub last night."

"How did you know?" John asked.

"Ben phoned me six thirty this morning if you ever did. I suppose he's quite worried, as you all must be. I did know that the will is being contested. They have got Jones and Jones, top London solicitors, working for them."

Suddenly there was a shout at the door. "Can I come in?" It was Cart. "I thought it was your car went up by," he said.

Mr Knight shook his hand and continued. "Sarah, my dear, whatever happens, it will not affect what you have been left, as you are his kin, although if they win, there might not be as much money left at the end."

"Do you think they will win?" Cart asked.

"That all depends on if she is who she says she is. Even if she is, it depends on so many things. If she had just walked away, what is it, twenty-five years or more ago? Then she would have no claim at all. If she genuinely lost her memory, then they look a bit more in her favour. But even then, Lord Trelivan always thought she would return, but he never made any provision in his will for her. Plus, she has never contributed to the estate. So in my opinion, she hasn't got much going for her."

"I wouldn't have recognised her, but I don't think there's much doubt that she is who she says she is. Me and Miss Pollard saw her early this morning. She certainly remembered a lot about us." There was no doubt in Cart's mind about who she was.

"When did you and Miss Pollard see her this morning? When you were checking the hay?" Sarah asked, laughing all over her face. She got a big kick under the table from Julie.

"How do you mean, dear? I don't have any hay." Cart was looking puzzled.

Both girls had a touch of the giggles. Sarah managed to straighten her face. "I feel quite sorry for her," she said. "She seemed a nice lady, and perhaps she deserves something."

"Let's not get too hasty." Mr Knight said, "I'm going to London on the train tomorrow to meet their solicitors and do a bit of digging. I'll give you an update if you let me have your number." Sarah wrote the phone number down on a piece of paper and handed it to him.

"Thanks. I'll be off, now. Make sure nobody worries, and I'll be in touch as soon as I can." They all shook hands and Mr Knight left.

Cart soon followed. "Oh, what about the hay?" he said.

"Did you want some for the harvest festival or something?"

"Oh, no, that's fine," Sarah replied, holding back the giggles.

Fred spent the whole of the day with George. And in the evening he went for a long walk with Julie. It seemed quite calm now that the harvest had finished. They had walked up around the meadow, lay on the ground by the pool, and kissed and cuddled for a while. Then they walked a bit more. On the way back they ended up in the shed. Fred was lying down on his back in the hay, Julie lying on her side looking down at him.

"What are you going to do now harvest has finished?" she asked.

"I don't know. I suppose I will have to look for a job."

"I suppose I should as well, but I don't want this to end. Do you still have the same dream as you did when we first came up here?"

"Of course, I do. I love George to bits, and I dream every night about helping people like him. But you can't live on dreams."

"I do love you, what did I call you, my Freddie kindness. Come here and check the hay, and I promise you I'll do everything I can to help you make your dream come true."

The following day after breakfast, Miss Pollard came around on her bike. "Morning all," she shouted, "just thought I would pop around and let you know I saw Lady Trelivan this morning. She and Rupert have gone back to London today."

"Did you recognise her?" Sarah asked.

"Not at first, but the more I listen to her, the more I do, if that makes sense."

"Did she know my mother well?"

"Oh, yes, dear, she knew her well. She knows about her

husband and your mum, and she was genuinely sad to hear about your mum's accident."

"That's nice to hear. I do feel a little bit sorry for her."

"I think we all do. It's that wretched Rupert that's the problem."

"Anyway, changing the subject, you and Cart seem to getting along well."

"We always have, dear, but we both lost a great friend. It seems to have brought us closer together, and who knows? We might only want one cottage."

Julie came into the conversation. "Have you been checking the hay?"

"Checking the hay, dear? What do you mean? Cart hasn't got any hay."

Julie now wished she had kept quiet. "Um, oh, I thought being a blacksmith he had a horse."

"Oh, no, dear, he hasn't had a horse for years. Well, I must be off; Oh, if you want a hand with the harvest festival, you know where to find us."

"Yes, checking the hay," Sarah whispered in Julie's ear as they waved good bye.

George made his way over to the barn; the others sat down out on the patio.

John suddenly realised he hadn't thanked Fred and Julie for their help during harvest. "You must think me awful. I haven't thanked the pair of you for all your help with the harvest. We would have struggled without you."

"Don't mention it; it's been a real pleasure. I've loved every minute of it, and I'm sure I speak for Julie." Fred reached out his hand and John shook it firmly.

"Have you got any plans for the future?" Sarah asked. "Of course, you're welcome to stay here for as long as you like; we would both miss you deeply if you went."

"We can't stay forever. It wouldn't be right. You pair

don't get any privacy, and you'll have children one day, and then you won't want us around." Julie, realising what she had said, reached across and held Sarah's hand and repeated softly, "You will have children one day."

"You're such a dear friend," Sarah said as she squeezed her hand. "Will you and Fred live together?"

"I hadn't thought about it, but I hope so, if we find somewhere."

"Your friend Andrew might not be impressed if you live in sin."

"Oh, I don't worry about that."

"John would love to have Fred working on the farm permanently. Whatever he does, if it doesn't work out there's always a place here."

"Fred has got a dream and I promised I would help make it come true." Julie told them all about Fred's dream.

"That's wonderful," Sarah said. "I would love to help, if that's ok."

"And you can count me in." John didn't want to be left out.

"That's great. I would love for you both to help. Quite frankly, I haven't got a clue where to start."

"Nor do I, but I think you should ask as many people as possible for help and you are bound to get a few suggestions." Sarah was getting quite excited about the idea.

"Steady on, Sarah. It's what Fred wants to do; it's his baby. You must let him do it his way." John could see Sarah taking over.

Fred was more than happy with her suggestions. "Oh, no, that's fine. I would love as much input as possible from both of you. And you, of course," he said, putting his arm around Julie.

"Right, then," said John, "let the dream begin. Sarah and Julie, one of you get a paper and pen and we can put all the suggestions down. Then Fred can mull them over."

They both went off and returned with pen and paper. "I don't know how high you're going to aim, and I don't want to put the mockers on it before you start, but I think you have to be realistic." John was just coming down to earth after his initial thoughts.

"Yes, I know exactly what you are saying. I have to earn money as well as doing this. That's why I've always been afraid it will remain a dream." Fred, too, had come down to earth.

"Hark at the pair of you, defeated before you start. Julie made a promise, and what Julie says, Julie does. Now, come on. Sarah and I are going to take notes. The first thing we have to do is decide why you want to do this."

"That's quite easy. I see how happy George is, and I think there are people like him that don't have the freedom he has. Some of them must live in towns and cities and never go outside. You imagine what it must be like for the parents as well." Fred looked at John and Sarah. "Imagine what your life would be if George couldn't run free."

"I know, we are so lucky. I know before you came and stayed, George would tire me out. Sometimes it would get really stressful, and I know when Mum was alive, it was hard for her to cope. We only had a small garden. She would have kittens when he used to wonder off." Sarah new exactly where Fred was coming from.

Julie had an idea. "What about if you raised some money and somehow offered cut-price holidays on the farm? We could entertain them." She paused for a moment, then continued. "I feel awful. I don't know what to call people with George's problem."

"Don't feel bad, Julie dear. George is my brother, and I don't know what to say is wrong with him. He's not ill, he's not got a disease, he's not under the doctor. So what is wrong with him?"

"This is part of the whole problem. I have read a little about it, and they have always called it Mongoloids, but there are two things and I wouldn't know one from the other. There is Down's syndrome and there is autism, but I don't think there is much known about either." Fred had obviously done some research.

"What do you think of Julie's idea, Sarah?" asked Fred.

"I think it's brilliant. Perhaps we should rope some of the villagers in and then see where we go from there."

"I think you should set goals and then it has to happen. So my suggestion, for what it's worth, is five families for a short break at Christmas. All those in favour, put their hand up."

"Hang on," Fred said, "where they going to stay?"

"You have just over three months to work it out, and I know you will, because you really want it to happen. And I love you to bits, my Freddy kindness."

"That doesn't sort out a job for you or somewhere to live. I have a suggestion, and if it is only temporary, so be it. We have the extra ground down at Stony Moor Mine. I want to put the suckle cows down there. My plan is to build the herd up to about a hundred and keep them down there without using much fertilizer. Try and let the wild flowers grow, try and keep it as a place of tranquillity. Of course, I will have to run the rest of the farm more intensively, except Julie's Meadow, that is. The point is, it will take a very special person to run the herd. Sometimes it will be quiet, sometimes busy. They would be their own boss and fit the work in to suit themselves. I would like that person to be you. And as for accommodation, you stay here until something comes along."

"I don't know what to say," Fred said. The one thing he loved in farming was Red Devon cows.

"You don't have to give me an answer now. Just think about it."

"Oh, I have already. I would be delighted to accept." He reached across and shook John's hand.

"What about you, Julie? What are we going to do about you, send you off to Plymouth to work?" Sarah said, smiling all over her face.

"No chance of that, I couldn't possibly be parted from you lot. I will have to find something local. Someone in the village must want someone to do something. I can cook or clean."

"John, you know, when they read the will, Mr Knight said the land at Stony Moor Mine and its buildings. What buildings?" Sarah asked.

"I don't know," John replied. "There is an old mine building down there somewhere. Perhaps we should go and have a look."

"Do you know where to look?"

"I know it's down by the river somewhere. Cart would know; he used to work there. That's where he learnt his trade."

Sarah was feeling quite inquisitive. "Come on, let's go and ask him."

Fred went over to get George and they all went off to the blacksmiths shop. Cart had just finished shoeing a horse.

"What you all up to?" He looked quite pleased to see them. "Come on in the cottage. Miss Pollard's indoors. She'll be pleased to see you all." They went indoors and told Cart why they had come around. They sounded so excited, it reminded Miss Pollard of Enid Bliton's famous five.

"Bloody hell," Cart said, "I haven't been down there for years, nor has anyone else that I know of. The mine captain's house was down there, a big stable and a blacksmith's shop. I loved it down there, but when the mine closed, it just got left. It's a long way down. I suppose it just got neglected."

Miss Pollard said, "You know, Lady Trelivan lived down there as a child."

"Was she well to do?" Julie asked.

"She was the mine captain's daughter. Her mother died when she was very young. Her father brought her up, and then when the mine closed, her father went to Canada. She went stay with Mrs Roberts at the post office. Her father was going to send for her, but he never did."

"Funny that," Cart said, "she always used to talk about it. But when we saw her the other day, she never mentioned it."

"Perhaps she couldn't remember. After all, she had lost her memory for a long time." Miss Pollard didn't read much into it.

"Will you come down there with us?" John asked.

"I would love to, but I don't think I could walk all that way; not and get back anyway." Cart was sounding disappointed.

"What about if we got the tractor and trailer? We could all ride down in the trailer."

"Bloody good idea, Fred," Cart said. "Olive can come as well."

"Olive? Who's Olive?" Sarah asked.

"Oh, Miss Pollard, to you, dear." All the years they had known her, they never knew her Christian name.

John and Fred went to get the tractor, and the others waited at the blacksmith's and told them all about what Fred wanted to do. "He is a great guy," Cart said, "you can count on me and Miss Pollard to give you as much help and support as we can."

It wasn't long before they came back with the tractor and trailer. They had put some bales of straw down both sides of the trailer for them to sit on. They all climbed aboard and off they went. "Exciting this, isn't it?" Miss Pollard said.

"Is it better to go up the lower lane or up across the fields and then down by the quarry?" John asked Cart.

"That was always the way, up the old lane. I don't know

what it's like, mind. I don't think anyone has been there for years."

It was quite surprising how good the lane was, under the circumstances, Yes, there were trees branching out over the lane, and they had to duck from time to time. Once they reached the old quarry, which was also the mine entrance, the lane took a sharp turn to the left, heading down through a wood towards the river. It wasn't a neat planted wood; it was an overgrown mess of self-sown ash, sycamore, a few oaks and plenty of brambles. You could see why nobody ever came down there.

As they came to the end of the lane, the whole area opened up. Although it was overgrown, it was nothing like as bad as the wood they had just driven through. As they looked across the opening, they could not believe their eyes. They could see a largish, square, stone-built house with some large granite steps going up to the door. To the side of the house, probably fifty feet away, was a very large building. It must have been a hundred and fifty feet long. John drove the tractor into the middle of the clearing and stopped, and they all got off.

Cart had a tear in his eye, as it brought back all his memories of working down there. "Bloody hell," he said, "it's in remarkable condition, considering how long it's been."

"How long?" Fred asked.

"How long ago would you say, Olive?" Cart was scratching his head. "I think it must be forty years," he said.

Miss Pollard said, "I know it didn't last long after the first war so you must be right; it has to be forty years."

"Bugger me, that makes us old, doesn't it, Olive!" Cart exclaimed.

"Speak for yourself," she replied.

"Come on, let's have a look around," Sarah said rather excitedly. They walked over to the house, slowly pushed the door open and crept in, half excited and half frightened. The house was completely empty; the windows were rotten, but still had most of their glass intact. The house and long building had a slate roof which was in remarkably good condition.

"What was the long building used for?" Fred asked Cart.

"Up that far end, let me see, is it five or six? We can count the doors in a minute, but I'm sure it's six stable blocks. Then next to that, where the big double doors are, was the cart shop. That's where they mended the carts in its heyday. They even made them there. Then down this end are lodgings. There would be fifty or more people sleeping there."

"Let's go and explore some more." Sarah was still sounding excited. "Do you think we could turn this in to your dream?" she asked Fred.

"It would take a lot of work, but it would be perfect, if that's all right with you and John."

"Of course, it is. We would be delighted and I'm sure we can get plenty of help."

They all got to the large doors by the cart shed and pulled them open as they went inside. "Look, what's that?" Cart shouted. In around the corner was a car. "How did that get here? It's not that old, is it?" he asked.

"No, I think it's a nineteen fifty-nine coupe." Fred was into cars. "Look, it has a broken headlight and the grill has been all smashed in. It's obviously been in an accident."

"Let's have a look inside." John opened the door as he said it. He picked something up off the floor. "It's a pay packet. It looks like one from the estate."

"Let me see," Sarah said, holding out her hand. "It has Sid Rogers's name on it. He's the head gardener."

"It can't be his car," Cart said, "he can't push a wheelbarrow in a straight line, leave alone drive a car."

"You know what this is," Fred brought the whole tone

down to earth as he turned to Sarah. "This is the car that ran your mother down, and I don't think we should touch anything. We have to get the police."

Sarah walked around the car and looked at the damaged front. "Oh God," she said, "why? Oh why? Who does it belong to?" She started to cry. "We must find who put it here, we must, we must." She turned to John and Fred, "Please help me find out whose car it is. Please," she said, drying her eyes.

"Of course, we will. But first we must get the police, and I think you girls should go back to the farm," John said, leading Sarah over to the tractor.

Miss Pollard, always thinking positively, said "I'll go with the girls and phone PC Roberts. Cart, you can stay with Fred, and John.

"Come on, George," Sarah said, "you must come with us."

While they were gone, Cart told Fred and John more about when he used to work there. "Good old days they were, but you probably only remember the good parts, and not the hard work and long days. Do you know, before my time they had a hundred and fifty horses here? They used to hire them out to other mines. That's why they bought the big block of land down here. Then, I believe when the First World War broke out, they commandeered a lot of them. I think we had about fifteen when I was here."

"What's that large building there in the woods?" Fred asked. About thirty yards into the woods was a large steel building about eight foot square. It was like a large cube.

"That was the old dynamite store," Cart remembered. "We should check that out if you are going to do some work here. If there was any dynamite left, it would be old and wet, and that's a recipe for disaster."

"Shall we have a look now while we are waiting?" Fred said, making his way towards the building.

When they got there, Fred was all for yanking the door open. "Not so hasty, young man," Cart shouted. "If there is something in there, a sudden movement could set it off. Look, there is no lock, so we need a piece of wood to just gently prise the door open."

Fred picked a large straight branch that was lying on the ground nearby and handed it to Cart.

Cart managed to get one end of the branch in the bottom corner and gradually opened the door very slowly.

Fred could not believe how someone so big and strong could put so much power into something, yet make it look so gentle. They both gasped in horror as the door opened wide, for there inside was a skeleton. There were bits of rope, some around the skeleton, some on the floor. There were also bits of clothes covering parts of the skeleton. It was obvious it had been there for a very long time.

"Who do you think it is?" Fred said to Cart. Just the thought of someone being left there to die was making him quite emotional.

"Bugger if I know," came the reply. "It's obviously a woman, judging by what's left of her clothes; she has a locket around her neck. Hadn't better look at it though. We better wait for the police. Good job the women went back to the farm; would not have done them a lot of good to have seen her."

John suggested that he go up to the farm to show PC Roberts the way down.

It seemed like ages before they arrived. When they did arrive, John and PC Roberts were on the tractor, and his bike was on the trailer. "You better come over here first," Cart shouted. They made their way over to where Fred and Cart where standing.

PC Roberts, trying to play the detective, asked, "Does anyone recognise her?"

"What a stupid bloody question," Cart said. "How many bloody skeletons do you think we know? Don't you think you should have got someone from Tavistock to come out?"

PC Roberts lifted his helmet. "I think you might be right; we have a major incident here. Now, I don't want you to say anything to anyone about this for the moment. And when we determine the time of death, I will have to ask you for your whereabouts to eliminate you from our inquiries."

"You silly bugger, no wonder they didn't want you in Tavistock. They gave you a push bike and sent you out here. She must have been dead for about twenty years or more." Cart was quite annoyed to think he had just come himself without informing Tavistock, even though they didn't know about the skeleton at the time.

"Is there a phone in the house?" PC Roberts asked.

He was now really getting under Cart's skin. "No," he shouted, "you will have to go up to the farm house. And don't forget to tell them about the car."

"Come on," John said, "jump on the tractor and I'll drive you up to the phone."

PC Roberts climbed onto the tractor. "Now, I am leaving you in charge," he said to Cart, "don't let anyone touch anything while we're gone, and make sure you keep members of the public away." They drove off up the lane.

"That silly bugger makes me mad," Cart said. "We should stop paying our rates as long as that silly bugger is our policeman."

"Did he investigate Sarah's mum's death?" Fred asked.

"No, they had a team up from Plymouth to investigate the robbery as well, but the trouble is, they left a lot of the foot work to that silly fool."

Up at the farm house PC Roberts was on the phone.

They had told the girls what had been found. "This is PC Roberts here. We have two major incidents out here, and I need immediate back up."

"Is he for real?" Julie said.

You could tell by listening to one side of the conversation that whoever was on the other end just wanted him to say what was going on. After about ten minutes, he managed to explain what they had found.

PC Roberts walked back down to the old buildings, and John waited to show the sergeant the way when he arrived. He did not seem to be waiting long, when the blue Ford Anglia drove in to the yard with its blue light flashing. "Can I drive down there?" the sergeant asked.

"It's a bit rough, but I think you should be all right. I can take you down on the tractor, if you would sooner," John said.

"No, that will be fine. If you just show me the way, and then if you don't mind waiting for forensics, they are coming up from Plymouth, and I would be grateful if you could show them the way."

Forensics arrived quite quickly, and they followed John down to the old buildings. When they got there, they split into two teams – one concentrating on the skeleton and the other on the car.

The team working on the car were asking Cart and John questions as they went over the car with great care. It had already been explained to them that they thought it was the car that ran Sarah's mum down.

"Were there two people knocked down?" one asked.

"No, why?" Cart answered.

"Well, if you look here, there are hairs in the bottom of the grill, which you would expect. As the person was hit by the headlight, they would have fallen and then been hit by the grill. Now, if you look here under the wing, there is also hair. The head could not have been hit in two different places on the car."

"What would your explanation be for that?" the sergeant asked.

"I can't be sure without taking the hair back to the lab, but I think it is the same hair. I think this car knocked someone down, and then went back and ran over them again on purpose."

"My God, we are looking at murder. We thought at the time … if this is the car, and I am pretty certain that it is … that Miss Page got knocked down, then another car ran over her. We never thought about it being the same car." The sergeant sounded as shocked as the rest.

"We have found a registration document in the glove compartment, along with some more pay packets," another of the forensic team said. The sergeant took it from his hand. "Someone in Plymouth is the register keeper. That will give us somewhere to start," he said.

They walked down to the team by the skeleton. "Any clues?" the sergeant asked.

"Only this," one of them said as he held up a locket. "There is a picture and an inscription inside. I can't read what it says, but I'll clean it up a bit in a minute. Then I can work it out. The person was tied up here and gagged, and I assume left here to die."

"So would it be fair to say we are looking at two murders, about twenty years apart," the sergeant asked.

"That about sums it up," one of the forensic men said. "I'll work out the inscription. Before we go, we will get the skeleton taken to the morgue and the car taken to our workshop in Plymouth. They will probably send a detective up from Plymouth in the morning, but until then it's over to you, sergeant."

The forensic man looked at John. "Have you any bicarb at the farm?" he asked.

"I would think so. I'll take you up there, if you like," he replied.

"No, you all go on. We will finish down here and then we will meet you up there, if that's ok with you," the man replied as he carefully put the remains of the clothing and rope into bags.

Everyone was up in the kitchen, except for George, who was over in the barn with the owl. It was like the owl understood everything that was going on.

Back in the kitchen, they all sat down and had a cup of tea and waited for the sergeant and forensic men. John had put the tub of bicarb on the table.

When the sergeant and the forensic team got to the house, the man with the locket asked for the bicarb and a cup of water. "All modern science," he said, "but you can't beat this." He carefully removed the picture from the back of the locket, and dropped the locket in to the bicarb and water. "I don't suppose anyone recognises the picture, do they?" he asked.

Miss Pollard stared at it on the table for quite a long time. "Yes, I do," she said softly, "and I know what it will say on the inscription."

"What?" Sarah gasped.

"It will simply say, "I will send for you." It's the locket Lady Trelivan's father gave her before he went to Canada. Oh, my God, I feel quite faint. Can I have a drink of water, Sarah dear?" she asked as she flumped down in the chair.

"Who do you think is responsible?" Fred asked. "Do you think the same person is responsible for both?"

"Would not have thought the same person," said the sergeant. "Too many years have elapsed between them."

"Don't be so bloody sure," Cart said. "I bet that Rupert's behind it somehow, and if that is Lady Trelivan down there, who is the woman that he's with?"

"Where are they now?" the sergeant asked.

"In London," John replied.

"They're coming back tomorrow," Sarah said. "When we got back here this afternoon, Mr Knight phoned to say that they had all met at the solicitors. It was decided that they had no claim. But it was suggested that they meet the other executors of the will tomorrow in Tavistock."

"I don't suppose he knew what train they would be on," the sergeant was hoping.

"No, but he had arranged a meeting at the hotel in the square at twelve thirty."

"Look, I need you all to keep this quiet for the moment. We don't want them to get wind of this. We should, on the information we have now, be able to charge them with fraud and see where it goes from there. Now, we have to be off. PC Roberts will stay down there until the skeleton and car are removed."

"Sergeant, would it be possible for us to see him before you make the arrest? I think he owes Sarah an explanation. I also think if we confront him, he might admit everything, but if you just arrest him for fraud and he denies everything you would have to let him go. We could go to the meeting instead of the trustees. You can guard the door and listen to everything that is said." John desperately wanted to confront him after all the misery he had caused.

"You have been reading too many books. It's far better left to the professionals," he replied.

Fred thought he could do a bit of persuasion. "I know what you are saying is right," he said, "and I don't think anyone of us would doubt your capability, but for Sarah and John… the misery that man has put them through … I think someone should give them a chance to confront him. It wouldn't make much difference to you if you arrested them an hour later, would it?"

"It's not down to me. It will be a detective from Plymouth that will make the decision. We will only be there as backup, but I will put it to him and let you know in the morning."

The sergeant put his helmet on as he left the kitchen and made his way to his car. Miss Pollard still couldn't believe that the woman that was with Rupert wasn't Lady Trelivan. "How did she know so much about us? She knew things Rupert wouldn't have known," she said.

"That's been puzzling me as well," Cart said, "but when you think of it, when she was talking to us, we were giving her the answers in a roundabout way. And she never once mentioned Stony Moor, yet there was never a day went by without Lady Trelivan mentioning it."

"She knew that Ben in the pub was my second cousin. How she could have known that? I just don't know." Miss Pollard was still confused.

"You told her, that's why," Cart said. "She said, "Let me see, isn't Ben related to you?" and you said, "Yes, he is my second cousin." Then she repeated it as if she knew."

"Now we know why Rupert wanted to get his hands on the farm; it would have been the only way he could get rid of the evidence," John thought.

With that, the phone rang. It was Mr Knight. "I have done a bit of digging," he said. "I don't think Rupert's companion is who she says she is. I have been to the club he used to visit, and they told me about a medium he was friendly with. I have tried to contact her, but she is not around. With the description they gave me, I am sure it is her. She has only just come out of prison after serving a twelve-month sentence for deception. Her name is Rosemary Gould."

Sarah explained to Mr Knight what had happened and how they had asked to see Rupert first.

"I will have a word, if that's what you want. Are you sure

it won't be to upsetting for you?" he asked.

"It might be upsetting, but I do need answers and I think this is the best way to get them."

"Well, if you are sure. I will be back some time tomorrow and I will look out and see you. I have some other news; you are going to be a wealthy young lady. So I'll say good night and see you tomorrow."

No one had realized the time until they looked out and it was quite dark. "We must be off," Cart said.

"I'll drop you back in the car," Fred said, taking his keys out of his pocket.

"Oh, no, don't bother with that. It won't take us five minutes. The walk will do us good," Cart replied.

"What about you, Miss Pollard?" John asked. "It's quite a long way out to your place."

Miss Pollard went quite red. "Oh, I'm spending a few days with Cart until things get sorted. He's been very kind to me," she replied.

Sarah whispered to Julie, "I bet he has. Do you think he's checking the hay?" she said with a giggle in her voice.

After they had gone, Sarah went over to the barn to get George. Fred remarked that no one had yet been to pick up the skeleton or the car, and that PC Roberts was still down there. John thought they should go down and see if he was all right.

"Have you got a flask?" Julie asked. "You could take him down a drink. It must be lonely down there."

John went to the cupboard and got the flask. Julie filled it up with tea, and Fred and John made their way down to PC Roberts. As they approached, there seemed to be no sign of him.

"Look over there," Fred said. PC Roberts had his back against a tree. You could just see he had his truncheon in his hand. "I think he is quite frightened," Fred continued.

"Shall we have a bit of fun," John said in an excited school-boy voice.

John picked up a small stone and tossed it down towards the skeleton. PC Rogers turned around and looked around the tree. He held his truncheon out straight like a gun. "Who's there?" he shouted. "Armed police; no one move."

"It's only us," John shouted.

"Who's "us"?" came the reply. "Say your names."

By this time, Fred and John were over beside him. "Oh, it's you two. You can't be too careful, you know. You never know who's around," he said.

"If I didn't know better, I would say you were afraid," John said, producing the flask from his pocket.

"Me afraid? No chance. I'm an officer of the law; no one would try to tackle me," he said, as he took the flask out of John's hand. "This is much appreciated."

With that, lights were seen coming down the lane. It was a Land Rover and trailer to pick up the car. Following that, there was a van to collect the skeleton. "Will you be all right now if we go on up?" John asked the PC.

"Of course, why shouldn't I be?" he replied.

"If that's the case, we'll bid you good night, and if you leave the flask there, we can pick it up in the morning," John said, as he and Fred made their way back towards the lane.

The following morning, a detective inspector, Brian Bolt, rang from Plymouth. "Mr Knight has been speaking to me," he said, "and he has told me what you want to do. I am prepared to go along with it, but the first sign of trouble and we will be in like a shot. Now, when you park, make sure your cars are out of sight. You must be in the hotel by eleven thirty to see my people, and they will tell you what is going to happen."

They were all getting quite excited. Sarah was quite apprehensive about the whole thing, though. She was glad she would finally know what happened to her mum and why. But sad it was all being brought up again. "I don't know if I can go through with it," she said to John.

"You don't have to. You can stay home and we'll go," John replied. "If you think it's going to upset you, I would much rather you stayed at home."

"I want to go, yet I don't. Does that make sense?" Sarah turned to Julie. "Will you stay home with me?" she asked.

"Of course, I will. I didn't want to go. I was going ask if you wanted me to stay and look after George," she replied.

"I had better go down and see if Cart and Miss Pollard are coming," John said. "We better leave about quarter to eleven to make sure we don't run into them."

"Mind they aren't checking the hay," Julie said as John went out of the door.

Cart and Miss Pollard were both going. So John and Fred picked them up on the way. They arrived in Tavistock and parked around the back of the market and made their way over to the hotel. As they got to the hotel, there was a doorman there to meet them. "Good morning, madam. Good morning, sirs," he said on their arrival.

They entered the hotel and were greeted by what looked like the receptionist, but was in fact a lady police officer. "Are you Sarah?" she asked Miss Pollard, looking rather puzzled at her age.

"Oh, no, not me, dear," she replied.

John explained how Sarah was feeling and how they thought it best if she didn't come.

"Well, it's a bit late to change things now, but you should have let us know. We only agreed to this so she could put things to rest."

"This will put things to rest for her, you can rest assured of that," John replied.

The officer explained that all the staff were police officers, and how there was a police officer in the room pretending to be one of the executors of the will.

They made their way into the room; it was laid out with a large table running down the middle, with ten chairs on each side. They were all told to sit down one side. They sat and waited for Rupert to arrive.

When Rupert and the lady who they now knew to be Rosemary Gould arrived, they were shown to the room where they were all sitting. Rupert was somewhat flabbergasted to see them sitting there when they entered the room.

"What's going on?" he said. "We are supposed to see the executors, not you lot."

"I would sit down," Cart said, "you might find this a bit more interesting."

"Oh, and what could you say that would interest me?" he replied.

"If you sit down, we can explain," Cart said with a voice of authority.

The pair of them sat down opposite. "Now, who's going to start? I think it should be you, John." Cart had made his mind up he was going to be the chairperson and get things moving.

John looked at Rupert. "We have found your car," he said. "You know, the one you knocked Sarah's mum down with. You know the one that you murdered her with."

"What car? I don't know anything about any car, and you want to be careful what you say or my mother and I will sue you. Now, if you don't mind, we're off." Rupert was beginning to get agitated.

"Oh, I wouldn't go yet. There's a lot more to come," John continued. He turned to the lady beside him. "Did he tell you he murdered his mother, Rosemary? Oh, yes, we have found her body as well. We know you murdered two people, but what we don't know is why."

"You don't know I murdered anybody. The car could be anybody's. You have no proof." Rupert was now looking very frightened.

John looked at Fred for support. "Oh, we have proof, all right." Fred was sounding like a QC. "You don't think the person in Plymouth you bought the car off would sell it to you without knowing your name. And then, what was it your mother scratched on the door?"

"She couldn't have done; her hands were tied," Rupert shouted. He started to cry. "It was an accident," he said, "she wasn't meant to die."

"How could it have been an accident when you bound her up like you did?" Cart asked calmly.

"All she ever talked about was Stony Moor. How good she was as a child and how awful I was. I knew she used to go down there to get away from me. I followed her there one day. She was sitting on the top step of the house crying. When she saw me, she told me to go away. She said she had had enough. She was going to tell my father that I hit her. I caught hold her hand and dragged her up. We were on the top step, she fell backwards and banged her head on the bottom step. She didn't move. I knew I would get the blame, so I tied her up and hid her in the old dynamite shed."

John looked at Cart and asked, "Why didn't anyone look there when she went missing? Surely it would have been an obvious place to look."

"No one ever thought anything bad had happened to her," he replied. "We all thought she had had enough and just left. I would give anything to turn the clock back. I feel so guilty we didn't look for her."

"What about Sarah's mum? Why did you knock her down," John asked. "And why steal the wages?"

"Nosey cow, she was," Rupert said. "Always where she

shouldn't be. I told my father I wanted the car; he told me I had to raise the money myself. Do you know they used to do the wages on Thursday and leave them on the table until Friday afternoon? My father always went out with Cart Thursday afternoons, so the money was there for the taking."

"But you must have already had the car before you took the money," John said.

"I did. I collected the takings from the saw mill the night before, then I bought the car, then took the wages to replace the takings. But when I picked them up, that nosey cow was there. She told me to put them back or she would tell my father. I lashed out at her, and she ran off. I jumped in the car and went after her. I accidently knocked her down. I did honestly go back to see if she was all right. She stood up, so I went to drive off, but she just fell in front of me. You can see both deaths were complete accidents."

"I don't see it that way, nor will Sarah. Did you know she felt sorry for you when the will was read? And all the time you had killed her mother." John could hardly control his anger. "I hope they lock you up and throw away the key," he said.

"No one is locking me up. I will just tell the police you made all this up to frame me. I have friends in high places in London," he said.

With that, the door opened and inspector Bolt entered the room. "I think that's enough now," he said, and he arrested the pair of them.

While they were out, the vicar had come around to the farm to discuss the harvest festival. Julie and Sarah were sitting on the bench outside the front door. The owl was flying around the yard and kept landing on George's arm and taking off again; it was just like a couple playing a game. The robin was sitting on the arm of the bench with its head looking upwards, as if it was listening to every word that was said.

The vicar was absolutely flabbergasted when they told him where the others had gone. He wondered if they still wanted to go ahead with the harvest festival, which was only a fortnight away. The girls agreed. It would take their minds off everything else.

They also told the vicar about the plan Fred had, and how they had set a date when it was going to start.

"What plans have you made," he asked, "and where are you going to do it?"

"No, we have no real plans, and we want to alter the old mine building. We don't really know where to start." But there was one thing Sarah was sure of – that it would happen.

"Would you let me help? I'm sure a lot of the villagers would muck in. And please call me Andrew."

Andrew coming around certainly helped the time pass by. It didn't seem long before the others returned. Sarah got very upset as they told her what had happened. Andrew said that, although she found it upsetting, she would be glad she knew what happened in the long term.

Cart, Miss Pollard and Andrew left together. Julie followed them out into the yard. When she returned, Fred whispered into her ear, "I can tell you are up to something."

No one felt much like tea that afternoon. Sarah found it more upsetting to think her mum's death wasn't an accident. "I did genuinely feel sorry for that bastard. Now I could kill him," she sobbed on John's shoulder.

It was about half past eight when there was a knock on the door. "Please send them away." Sarah couldn't face any one.

"Oh, no, Mrs." Julie picked up a handful of candles. "We are going up to Julie's Meadow to put your mum to rest. Now come on."

Sarah reluctantly put her shoes and coat on. They went out in the yard and were greeted by Cart, Miss Pollard and Andrew. John whispered to Julie, "I knew you were up to something."

They made their way up to the meadow. The owl came all the way on George's shoulder, and even though it was nearly dark, the robin was sitting on a thistle which was growing tall beside the pool.

They all gathered around the pool. The sun was a glowing red setting in the distance. No matter what time of day you went there, there was something absolutely magical about the place. "If God made a garden, this is surely it," Julie said as she looked into the sunset.

Andrew offered up a prayer for Sarah's mum, and they all lit candles and placed them by the pool. "Can we sing "All Things Bright and Beautiful"," Sarah sobbed.

Julie held her hand and gently squeezed it. "We can do whatever you like," she whispered.

Andrew got everyone together. "Come on, you all know the words." The sound rang out around the valley. As they were singing, it fell in to darkness, and as you looked into the pool, there in the light of the candle was a reflection of an angel. Sarah looked in to the pool. "Good night, Mum. God bless. I know you will be always with me."

They left the candles burning and returned to the farm. "Everyone must come in for a drink." Sarah was feeling much better as she led them to the door.

The topic of conversation soon came around to Fred's dream. "We could turn the building down at Stony Moor into the holiday accommodation." Sarah was quite excited.

"Are you sure that will be all right?" Fred was all for that. "We would need planning permission."

"That's no problem." Cart had friends on the council. "I'm owed a few favours," he said.

"Has anyone thought who you are going to ask to stay when the time comes?" John said. "We know they are out there, but how do we find them?"

"It's early days, but a friend of mine in Bristol is helping a group of parents form an autistic society. That would be a good place to start."

"I think we have had an exhausting day. I think we should all have a good night's sleep and arrange a meeting with the village where we can discuss this and the harvest festival." Miss Pollard had had enough for one day.

When they had gone, John suggested bed.

Sarah caught hold Julie's hand and led her to the chair at the top of the table. "You three go on. I want a word with Julie a minute."

The three men went on to bed. "What's wrong? What is it?" Julie had a worried tone in her voice.

"Nothing is wrong. I want to know, do you think there is an angel up in Julie's Meadow?"

"What do you think? Some people will say it's the light playing tricks, some will say it's the shadow of the tree, and there are others who will say it's just imagination." Julie squeezed her hand gently. "It's for each of us to believe what we will."

"You haven't answered my question. Do you believe?"

"Yes, dear, I believe. I believe it's very close to you; it never appears when Fred and I are alone up there."

Sarah smiled. "That's probably a good job, with what you pair get up to."

Julie had the look of contentment on her face. "Nothing more than you would do, my dear. Now come on, time for bed."

Sarah stood up kissed her on the cheek. "Don't ever leave us, will you?" she said as they made their way up the stairs.

The next morning after breakfast they all went for a walk

down to Stony Moor. They were somewhat surprised to see Cart and Miss Pollard there. Cart was reminiscing to Miss Pollard about the view that used to be there, but it was now lost due to the trees.

"Soon sort that out. Get old Bill Townsend down here with his chain saw." John wanted to get things started.

They all sat on the steps of the house looking out to where the view used to be. Cart could remember seeing the river.

Suddenly they heard someone shouting; it was Mr Knight. He was sweating profusely. "It's a long way down. I don't think I have ever walked so far. I wouldn't have bothered you, but I have some papers that need signing."

"We will come back up now." Sarah got up from the step and made her way to the lane.

Mr Knight was still sweating. "Do we have to walk up, or have you got some transport?"

"Shanks pony, I'm afraid." Cart was laughing. "A few days in the country would do you city folk the world of good."

They all left and made their way up the lane.

It was later that afternoon when Andrew called around to ask if they could come to the pub that night to discuss the harvest festival.

The meeting all went well. Everything was decided, who was doing what at the harvest festival. Bill Townsend, the log man, was in the pub. "John, you want to get him down and cut those trees down?" Cart said he would go down and show him which ones.

John went over and approached Bill.

"How much you paying me?" he asked.

Cart interrupted. "Paying you? You twisting old bugger, you should be paying John. Now here's the deal. You can have the wood, but they need two trailer loads of logs left down there. I'll let you know what length. And I'll be there to keep an eye on you, you old bugger, now shake on it."

Bill spat on his hand and held it out to John. "Bloody good nature I got," he said, as he shook John's hand firmly.

The harvest festival soon came around. John and Fred placed bales of straw around in a circle for people to sit on, and parked the bale trailer in the middle for the church choir to perform on.

Miss Pollard had made some sheaves of corn. Sarah helped her build a display with the sheaves and wheelbarrow loads of fruit and vegetables Sid Rogers had brought over from the estate gardens. Julie spent all day in the kitchen making pasties.

They were just finishing off the display, when a horse and cart came down across the field. Miss Pollard looked up. "It's Farmer Lane. Whatever does he want?" She greeted him politely, but you could tell something made her feel uncomfortable when he was around.

"Brought down a barrel of cider, Mrs. You can't have a do without a bit of cider."

"It's not that sort of do. It's the harvest festival. It's to thank God for a good harvest."

"The apples that made this cider last year was a good harvest. So stop being an old fuddy-duddy and give us a smile."

"Bloody old man," came from under Miss Pollard's breath.

"Why, Miss Pollard, I do believe I heard you swear," Sarah said with a smile.

"That man would make the vicar swear. Just leave the barrel there. I expect someone will appreciate it."

The evening was a great success. Julie had made over a hundred pasties. Cart was very impressed with them. He told Miss Pollard that he always thought her pasties were the best, until he had one of these. Of course, Fred had said it was the Aga that made the difference.

News must have got around about Gilbert Lane's cider, as nearly everyone brought a glass. Even Miss Pollard was seen drinking from Cart's glass.

Andrew said prayers, auctioned of all the produce, and announced what a great success it was.

Julie and Sarah had brought candles with them to light when everyone had gone. When the time came, Julie was nowhere to be seen. "Look over there by the barrel," John shouted. Low and behold, lying flat out on the ground was Julie.

"I only had a little drink-e and I think it's gone to my head. O, and my legs," she said as she tried to stand up.

"If we stand her up, I'll get my arm around her and help her back to the farm." That was Fred being practical.

"No, would you help her down to the pool and we can light some candles and sit for a while?" Sarah wasn't ready to go back.

John and Fred carried some bales and put them in a row beside the pool. They managed to get Julie on one. Sarah set the candles out and lit them and sat back with the others.

Julie had a real touch of the giggles. This was the first time she had ever had too much to drink. The most she had ever had before was two Babyshams. She couldn't stop talking.

Sarah was egging her on. "Tell us what you and Fred get up to here."

"Oh, I can't tell you that. Oh, no, no, no I can't tell you that," she said, waving her finger.

They stayed there for about an hour. Julie had started to sober up. There was no sign of an angel. Sarah thought Julie had frightened it away. But just as they were leaving, a silvery shape passed over Sarah. No one else saw it, but Sarah knew she did.

# Chapter 3

With harvest festival over, it was time to concentrate on getting the building ready for Christmas. Andrew had a lot of discussions with the four of them; he had also been in touch with his contact in Bristol. He had put an idea to them; he suggested that they run it as a business. He thought that if you do it as a charity, it might fold, as it could be difficult to raise the money to keep it going. It would be easier for the people to raise the money at the other end to send the people to stay.

All four of them thought that it was a good idea, as they could keep the price very modest. Sarah was adamant that the first one, at Christmas, would be free; she would cover the cost out of her inheritance, and she would also pay for the building materials for the building.

They asked Andrew if through his contacts he could find five deserving families to come at Christmas.

Nearly everyone in the village lent a hand, and an invitation for Christmas was offered to all of them. Even Julie's and Fred's parents came and helped; the four of them were coming for dinner.

Julie's parents kept pestering her about a job. "Don't keep on. I promise I will get a job after Christmas."

Cart had spent hours down with chainsaw Bill, the log man. With the trees felled, the views became spectacular. They had a large pile of wood beside the building for the fire.

Opening day was fast approaching. Fred had George beside him as he worked; he could now converse, although he was difficult to understand at times.

The stables had been converted into five individual sleeping quarters, each with two bedrooms and a bathroom.

Next to that was a kitchen, and then on from that was one long room and in the centre was a large fireplace which would take three-foot logs. Cart had put a large Christmas tree in one corner. Miss Pollard had come down and put up the decorations.

With all the building work finished, it was now time to make arrangements for the guests. "I think we should write up some sort itinerary," Julie suggested.

Sarah suggested they should give the place a name. They couldn't go on calling it Stony Moor mine buildings. Fred suggested George Page Lodge, because without George it would never have happened.

Sarah smiled. "Do you know, I think that's a good idea. But I think I prefer George Trelivan Lodge. We can get some signs made up tomorrow."

All the others said, in harmony, "I think that's wonderful," and in turn they all gave her a big kiss.

"It's getting really close, and we haven't done anything about food. That should be our first priority." Fred was worried no one had thought about that.

"We can't really do much until Miss Pollard lets us have numbers from the village," Sarah said. "Perhaps I'll give her a ring first thing in the morning. Then Julie and I will go over to Gilbert Lane's; he said he would let us have turkeys cheap."

John started to laugh. "You hadn't better take Julie over there. You know what happened last time she smelt his cider."

"Very funny, but not a bad idea. Do you think he will let us have some? I quite liked it. But I promise I will put lemonade with it next time."

"Oh, we know you liked it, all right." John was teasing her. "It was what you were saying was the problem. Poor Fred was so embarrassed."

She turned to Fred. "What did I say? I didn't embarrass you, did I?"

"Let's put it this way," Fred replied, "good job we were amongst friends."

Sarah had to have her bit of fun. "We still haven't tried the position you were talking about."

"Now I know you are teasing, because we haven't done anything you pair haven't."

"Would we tease you?" John was smiling at her as he said it.

George was even laughing. "Julie drunk," he said, then repeated it. "Julie drunk."

"George," she said "don't you pick on me as well. I thought you were my friend."

"I love Julie." He put his arms around her, "And big hug," he said.

Sarah's eyes started to fill up as she walked around and put her arms around both of them. "I love all of you," she said, "and I have never been so happy in my life."

They all went on to bed. Fred was lying in bed, and Julie was getting undressed in front of the window; the moon was shining bright through the window. Julie stood there naked. Fred shuddered as a cold shiver ran down his spine.

"What is it?" she gasped.

"That angel, it's here," he replied.

"Where?"

"Right there in front of the window. Just stand there for a minute, I just want to admire your beauty."

"You silly bugger," she said as she jumped on him.

He cuddled her in. "I think I have neglected you over the last couple of months, but I promise I will make it up to you."

"My dearest, dearest darling, you haven't neglected me. If anything, it's the other way around; I've neglected you. I don't think you know how much I love you. Some days, when I haven't seen you for a little while, my heart just flutters when you appear."

"You better see the doctor, you've probably got palpitations," he said laughing.

"Now you are teasing me again. I'm never going to tell you how I feel again."

"Cuddle right in close to me and I will tell you how I feel." She cuddled in until every bit of their naked bodies was touching. He stroked her hair. "I feel the luckiest man in the world. I feel you are the most beautiful thing in the world. I feel I will love you forever."

Julie interrupted him, "I feel something stirring that tells me you want to check the hay, and I feel that's what I want to do right now."

This was the first time they had made love indoors, but I doubt it would be the last.

The next morning, Andrew arrived with a list of people that were coming to stay. There were five people with disabilities similar to George's; three of them were girls and two boys, their ages ranged from fourteen to twenty-six. Two of them had sisters: one twelve and the other fifteen. Four of them had their mother and father coming with them, and one had just her mother.

"There is one other. Now, I know there is not room for her to stay, but this has made me feel guilty as hell. I have never done anything for her before. There is a girl called Jenny. No one knows how old she is; she was found wondering around Tavistock when she was about ten.

"The last fifteen years she has been living up at the monastery and she has never gone out. The nuns look after her, but since Sister Joyce died, I don't believe there is any love for her."

"So you should be guilty." Julie was going to give him a lecture. "Who's right about God, now, then he wouldn't have neglected her. He can't be everywhere. He thought you were taking care of things. When he realised you weren't, he introduced you to us. You never know that's why he might have sent George, because without George this wouldn't have happened. It just shows everyone has a purpose."

"I know you are right, but I'm sure he will forgive me. Oh, by the way, one other thing. Your guests arrive the day before Christmas Eve, which is the day of the carol service, and I wondered if we could hold it down at the buildings."

"I've spoken to Cart. He said he would light a bonfire if that was all right with you."

"Yes, that's fine. I'll try and get some lights today and put them on the fir tree that's left in the middle." John thought it would really brighten it up.

Sarah came off the phone to Miss Pollard. "Who can guess how many are coming to dinner?" She was quite excited.

John scratched his head. "I wouldn't be surprised if there were ten."

"You will be surprised when I tell you that thirty-five have said they are coming. Julie and I will have to concentrate on the food, now we only have four days." She turned to John. "Are you and Fred all right to finish off, while Julie and I go and start getting the food? We will need to take the pickup."

"That's fine. Where you going first?" John asked.

"I think we should go over to Gilbert Lane's to see what he has; he said he would give us a good deal. How many turkeys do you think we will need? There will be fifty-four or -five people in total."

Julie said, "If you had one turkey for a family of ten, then we would probably get away with five large ones."

"Come on, then, let's get over and see the daft bugger, as Miss Pollard calls him," Sarah said as she picked up the pickup keys.

"Just remember what Miss Pollard said; make sure he doesn't do you."

"I didn't know you could drive," Julie said as they drove out the gate. "When did you pass your test?"

"Which do you want me answer first, the fact that I can drive, or the bit that I haven't taken my test?"

"I don't think I want to know that."

They drove up the long rough track to get to the farm. "Just keep smiling, and we will get him eating out of our hands, and we will come away with a bargain," Sarah said laughing.

Gilbert came out to meet them. 'It's lovely to see two so pretty things," he said. "Now you can have the pick of the turkeys. How many do you want?"

"Five, if you can spare them," Julie quickly replied.

"Let's see what we can do. There are thirty in here. You pick what you want, the rest will go to Plymouth market tomorrow,"

He led them in to what was a very cold stone shed. It had a long slate bench with all the turkeys laid out on it. On the other side of the shed was another bench with geese on it.

"Now you pick," he said, "there are five nice fifteen-pounders here, look. Or a couple of twenty-pounders. Come on, you pick."

"What about three twenty-pounders and two fifteen?" Sarah said, feeling their breasts.

"They got nice breasts," Gilbert said. "I like nice breasts; they remind me of Miss Pollard. She had nice breasts. What did the old bat say about me, anyway?"

"Well, actually, she said we had to watch you like a hawk." Julie looked right at him and rolled her eyes as she said it.

"Hee, hee, hee, hee," he went, which was like a shricking laugh. "I used to pinch her on the ass, you know. It used to drive her mad."

He walked out of the shed and returned with of a large enamel bowl of yellow stuff.

"What's that?" Julie asked.

"That, my dear, is goose fat, for roasting your tiddies."

"Tiddies," Julie said looking startled.

"Yes, tiddies. You know, potatoes. Now, talking of tiddies, have you got yours? You need about three hundred weight. I've got some beauties."

"Yes, we'll have them, if you give us a good price." Sarah was trying to show she wasn't going to be a pushover.

"What about some cider?" Julie asked.

"I can't sell that. See, it's the duty on it. But what I can do is give you ten gallons and put a little on something else to cover it. What about ten gallons of apple juice? You can go in Tavistock and get some cloves and spices and make a nice mulled drink."

"That would go down well at the carol service with a mince pie," Sarah thought. "That will do, then. Now, let me know how much it is with our discount," Sarah continued.

"Right," he said, "here we go: five turkeys at one pound ten shillings each is seven pounds ten shillings; three hundred weight of tiddies, two and six a cwt, is seven and six; that's seven pounds seventeen and six. The cider should be three pounds, but we can't charge for that, so say six pounds for the apple juice. That's thirteen pounds seventeen and six, then there's the goose fat and the sweeds."

Julie interrupted. "We haven't got any sweeds," she said.

"Oh, you have to have some sweeds," he said, as he threw two bags in the back of the pickup. "Now, let me see, where was I? Fifteen pounds seventeen and six."

"No," Sarah interrupted, "thirteen pounds."

"Oh, yes, I tell you what. Give me eighteen pounds, and I'll throw the other bits in. How about that."

He held his hand out and Sarah shook it. "Deal," she said.

They loaded up the pickup and drove off. "If you think

about it," Julie said, those sweeds and goose fat were rather dear. I think we've been done."

"I think you're right. We best keep it to ourselves, though, or they will all laugh at us."

They went off to Tavistock and got the rest of the food, and dropped an order for mince pies into the baker's in the village on the way back.

When they got back to the farm, Julie's mum and dad were there. "We thought we better come over and see if there are any last minute jobs you need a hand with," Sarah's dad said.

"And look who's come to see you," her mum said, looking rather pleased.

It was Robert's mum. "Hello, dear. We thought after all that you were doing here, it would nice to come and see for ourselves."

"It is lovely to see you both," Julie replied.

"Yes, you too, dear. I said to Mr, it's no good bearing grudges. What will be, will be, and if you found love somewhere else, so be it."

"I don't know what you mean." Julie was beginning to feel a little uncomfortable.

"Well, dear, you know, you breaking off your relationship with Robert for someone else."

Julie looked quite angry. "You don't know, do you?" She turned to her mother. "You haven't told her, have you? How could you? Why didn't you?"

Sarah's mum was wishing she hadn't brought Robert's mum and dad with them, as she said, "I thought it for the best."

Sarah was really getting mad. "Best? Best for who? Certainly not me."

Robert's mum didn't know what was going on. "Will someone please tell me what this is all about?" she screamed.

"I will tell you, all right. Yes, I was going to finish with Robert, because I wasn't sure I loved him and he never showed me any affection. And do you know why? He's queer. That's why."

His mum gasped. "Whatever do you mean?"

"I mean just that. He prefers men to women. He only went with me to cover it up."

"I don't believe a word you are saying. It's a good job you didn't get married, you spiteful girl. How could you come out with such lies? You couldn't get more of a man; he's always fishing and rabbiting. We all know why you finished with him, so you could shack up with someone else. You are no more than a slut."

Julie started to cry. She turned to her mother. "Why don't you say something? Are you just going to let her talk to me like that? This was the best time of my life and you had to ruin it. Why? Oh, why?"

She ran out of the kitchen and up the stairs to her bedroom.

Sarah was also quite upset. "I think you better go up to her," she said to her mum.

"I think it best if I drop you home," Julie's father said to Robert's parents, "and I'll come back later."

"Just, before you go, I would like to say something." Sarah wasn't going to let them go without them knowing what a great girl Julie was. "Julie has done a lot for me through my tragedy. She has even helped others with their outlook on life. When she came here, it wasn't to shack up with anyone. It was to help me with my loss. And I can assure you, she is neither a liar nor a slut. I hope you will be able to except that your son is gay, for your own sake and his. Now, I will bid you good-day," she said as she left the room.

Robert's mother put her hand on Julie's dad's shoulder as he drove them home. "Dom," she said, "is it true? Is our Robert gay."

Dom stopped the car and turned to face her. "Yes, it is true. We never told you, as we didn't want to upset you. But I wish we had. It would have been for the best."

"I just don't know what to say. That poor girl. What must she think of us? How did she find out?"

"She saw him with someone."

"Because he was with someone, that doesn't mean anything."

"It was what they were doing. I don't really want to go into it. I would sooner leave it to your imagination."

Dom started the car and drove on. Roberts's father had been rather quiet, but he suddenly sighed. "Where did we go wrong? Where, oh where?"

They had reached their house. Dom stopped the car. "You can't blame yourself," he said. "You have to except it, for Roberts's sake as well as your own. People look at these things differently now. There is not the stigma there was. I don't mind admitting I thought it disgusting when I first heard it, but I can accept it now."

"Do apologise to Julie for us. I hope she will forgive me for the things I said. I don't think I will ever forgive myself," Robert's mother said as she waved good-bye.

Back at the farm, Julie's mother had been up in the bedroom. Julie was laying face down, sobbing. She sat on the bed beside her and stroked her hair. "Oh, Julie dear, please forgive me. It was my idea not to tell; your father told me it would end in tears. If I could turn the clock back, I would. Why, oh why do I always manage to get it wrong?"

Julie turned around. "It was the things she called me. I'm not a bad person."

"Everyone knows that, dear. You are very caring. Now come on, dry your eyes. Your father will be back soon."

"You go on down. I'll be down in a minute."

— *133* —

She got to the door and turned back. "Where's Fred's bedroom?" she asked.

"He sleeps with me," Julie replied, expecting some criticising remark.

Her mum just smiled when she said, "He's not gay, then."

"No chance of that," she replied.

Sarah went up to see Julie. "Don't be too hard on your mum. Mums don't always get it right, with all their best intentions."

"I know she meant well, but how do you think it makes me feel? I know I went to see him to end it, but that's not the point. Anyhow, I forgive them now."

"What, all of them?"

Julie smiled. "Robert's parents will have to wait until tomorrow, and as for Robert, I might consider it at Christmas. I hope when I have children I'll be a bit more understanding."

Sarah also started to smile. "The way you pair carry on, that might be sooner than you think."

"Oh, no: we take precautions."

Sarah sounded inquisitive, "What precautions?"

"I keep my fingers crossed."

"Wrong part of the body, my dear."

"I'm only joking. We use something most times. That's enough about us. What about you pair?"

Sarah went very quiet. "Haven't done it since I lost the baby. I feel sorry for John. I want to. God, I want to. I just can't relax. It's funny. It just doesn't feel right. I know it's stupid, but it seems disrespectful to my baby."

"My dear, Sarah." Julie hadn't realised how much it affected her. "You never said anything. I wish you had told me."

"Why would I worry you? Anyhow, it's a bit personal."

"I'm your therapist, that's why. I could help you."

"I know what to do. I don't need any help. Anyway, it

was only a few months ago you asked me if you were doing it right; now you're an expert?"

They both laughed. "Come on," Julie said, "we have got work to do. Our guests arrive tomorrow." As they went down the stairs, she whispered into Sarah's ear, "It will be all right. Promise."

When they got into the kitchen, Julie's mum was there, looking anxious. She put her arm around Julie. "Do you forgive me?" she asked.

"This time I do, but just remember what you used to say to me. Always tell the truth, no matter what, as the truth will always come out in the end."

Julie's mum was worried what Sarah would think of her. "I know I was wrong. I don't know what you must think of me, Sarah. I'm not like that, really."

"Oh, don't worry about me," Sarah said, "let's put it all behind us and look forward to the next few days. Shall we go down to the lodge and see what's left to be done?"

As they were walking down the track, Julie's father returned and caught them up. He put his arm around Julie. "They both send their apologies," he said.

"It might take more than a few words," she replied, "but we'll see."

When they got to the bottom by the lodge, Cart was there putting lights up on the tree that was left in the middle of the courtyard, outside the lodge. "What do you think of this?" he said. He had made a large fire basket. It was v-shaped, about three feet long, it had crossed legs, which stood about two feet tall, and the basket was about two feet deep.

"Oh, Cart," Sarah said, "this is Julie's mum and dad."

Julie's dad put out his hand. "I'm Dom, and this is Molly," he said, pointing to his wife. Cart shook his hand firmly. Dom turned to Sarah. "And that's the same to you madam, it's Dom and Molly."

"This is Olive," Cart said as Miss Pollard came towards them.

"Good afternoon," she said. "I just came over to see how the girls got on with Gilbert."

"Very good," Sarah quickly replied. "We had him eating out of our hands. We had real bargains. Just out of curiosity, how much is goose fat?"

"About a shilling a pound, depending on quality. I hope you didn't pay any more."

"Oh, no, we had it all as a job lot." Julie was finding it hard to keep a straight face.

Cart had got twelve old granite gate posts; he had made two rows of semicircles in front of the fire. "They are great seats, but I'm afraid they might be a bit hard to sit on, and a bit cold," he said.

"I think they're lovely. What we want is some cushions," Sarah said as she sat down on one.

"What about some bags of hay? There's plenty of soft hay up in the shed at the top of the…" Fred's voice gradually got quieter as he realised what shed he was talking about. "… field."

"We've got some Hessian potato bags up in the barn. They would do. Fred and Julie could fill them tonight," John said with a big smile on his face.

"Tiddy bags, you mean," Sarah said, laughing.

"What a good idea. We could sew the tops when we get back." Julie was up for that.

It had started to get dark, so they decided to call it a day. Everyone was quite excited to think the guests were coming tomorrow.

Fred, John, Julie, Sarah and George were sitting down having their tea. "We will have to work out some sort of a menu," Julie said. "We ought to do it for the whole ten days they are here. We will have to do some more shopping tomorrow."

They had their tea and done the washing up. George had gone over to the barn to see the owl. John had gone with him to get the potato bags.

"What a beautiful moonlight; it's quite romantic," John said, as he returned with the bags under his arm. "Here you are." He handed them to Fred.

Julie suddenly started to clutch her stomach and moaned in pain. "I don't think I can go," she said.

"My, whatever is it?" Sarah was concerned.

"I think it's just a cramp," Julie replied with a painful frown on her face.

"Fred and I will go," John said as he picked up the bags.

"Oh, I want Fred to stay with me, if that's all right. Would you mind going?" Julie said as she turned to Sarah.

"That's fine. Come on, John, we can take the pickup up across the field."

John and Sarah left and drove out the gate. As soon as they were gone, Julie jumped up. "Come on, let's go and see what George is up to," she said.

"I thought you weren't feeling well," Fred said, surprised.

"Who, me? Never felt better," she replied.

Fred was still confused. She had never been known to refuse an opportunity to go to the shed before. "I don't understand," he said.

"Let's just say it's me doing my bit for nature," she replied. "Now come on, let's go and see George."

John and Sarah got up to the shed, they opened the door wide and went in. The moon shone right in through the doorway. Sarah held the bags open and John pushed the hay in. As he pulled a clump out of the pile, it came away easier than he thought it would. He fell backwards and the hay shot up in the air and covered Sarah. "Oh, I'm sorry," he said as he got up and started to take the hay out of her hair.

Sarah started to fidget. "It's gone down inside my blouse," she said.

John gently put his hand inside her blouse to get it out. "I can't find any. I bet it's the seeds; they make you itch like anything."

"It's no good. It itches like hell. I will have to take it off and shake it out."

John was laughing at her, so she picked up a handful of hay and shoved it down his trousers.

She removed her blouse; John was reaching down inside his trousers to get the hay out. She dropped her blouse on the ground and stood facing him. Her breasts were firm in a low-cut lace bra. "Come here, let me" she said. She put her hand down and started to pull the hay out of his trousers. She whispered in his ear, "It's no good, you will have to take them off." John nervously removed his trousers. Even though it was something he had done in front of her a thousand times, he was quite embarrassed.

"God, I feel nervous doing this," he said.

"Me, too. I feel nervous and excited all in one," she said as she wriggled out of her tight jeans.

"What are you doing?" John asked in an excited voice.

Sarah had her hands behind her back, undoing her bra. "We are going to check the hay." She dropped her bra gently to the ground, and slowly removed her little lace panties. She stood there naked in the moonlight, her body glowing bronze.

"I forgot how beautiful you are," he said as he took her in his arms. They gently fell back on the hay. "Are you sure about this?" he whispered.

"I couldn't be surer," she replied as their lips met.

Back in the barn, George was having fun with the owl. Julie had found an old, large needle which was used for mending Hessian sacks. "This will be ideal for our cushions," she thought.

Fred was over with George. They got the owl to fly around the barn. Then it would swoop down and take bread from their hands. It was like the owl was playing with them; when you thought it was going to George, it would change at the last minute and go to Fred, then he would reverse the procedure. Julie came over and joined them.

"John and Sarah have been a long time," Fred said as he put his arm around her.

"That's a good sign," she replied.

"How do you mean?"

"Let's just say the angel is about tonight, and leave it at that. Now, I'll go in and put the kettle on. You pair come in when you're ready."

All three of them were in drinking tea when John and Sarah got back. Sarah was absolutely glowing when she walked in. She came right over to Julie and kissed her on the cheek. "Thank you," she said. She knew why Julie didn't go to the shed.

Sarah was pulling at her jeans and scratching her bum as she walked around the kitchen. "You got ants in your pants?" Fred said jokingly.

"No, it's hay in the knickers," she replied, "and if you excuse me, I must go and take them off," she said, walking out of the room.

Julie followed her to the bedroom. "Well, tell me about it," she said.

"All I'm going to say is your little plan worked. Do you know, I genuinely felt you were ill. It wasn't until after that I realised what you had done. I'm beginning to think you are a real angel."

The next morning was full of excitement. It was the day the guests were arriving. Sarah and Julie were going to work out a menu and do the last minute shopping.

The men were going to take some of the pigs and calves

down to the field beside the lodge so they would be easy for the guests to see.

Sarah and Julie were off out the door with a gigantic shopping list. As they got in the pickup, the postman arrived, "Can't stop and make you coffee this morning," Sarah shouted.

"No matter. I'm too busy anyway. Just one letter for Miss Julie," he replied as he handed her the letter.

"You've got a secret admirer, by the look of it. It's a proper letter," Sarah said, laughing.

Julie opened it. "It's from Robert's mother."

"Go on, then, read it out."

"It might be personal and private."

"It might be to everyone else, but not me. I'm your mate."

Julie opened the letter right out and started to read it as Sarah was driving them to the shops.

*My Dear Sarah,*

*How can you possibly forgive me for the things I said? I am so, so sorry. It was the total shock of learning about Robert. It's probably the worst thing a mother could hear. I truly know what a special girl you are, and how much you do for others. I also know that you would have to go a long way to find someone as loving and caring as Fred. When he was about seven or eight, he came down to our house. He had brought our cat back that had been kicked by a horse. You could tell then he was caring. We will have to except what our son is, and I hope he is man enough to apologise to you one day, for the way in which he used you.*

*I wish you and Fred all the best in the future and hope we can remain friends.*

*Wishing you all my love and a very merry Christmas.*
*Dorothy.*
*xxx*

"That's quite nice," Sarah said. "She thinks you're special, and I know you're special."

They went on into town and did the shopping. On the way back, they called in the baker's to get the mince pies and pasties for the carol service.

"How you going to cook five turkeys?" Joe the baker asked.

"Not quite sure yet," Sarah replied. "I hope Julie's mum will cook one. I think we can get two in the oven down the lodge, and one up the farm, and I was going to ask Miss Pollard to cook the other."

"Why don't you bring them over to me Christmas Eve all ready for the oven. Then I'll cook them Christmas morning. Plenty of room in my oven."

"Are you sure?" Sarah thought it would be great.

"I wouldn't have offered if I wasn't sure. They will be in early and you can pick them up about twelve." Sarah leaned over the counter and kissed him on the cheek. "Thanks for that," she said.

Julie also leaned across the counter and gave him a kiss. "That's one from me as well," she said.

Joe had a big smile on his face. You would think he had just had the best Christmas present ever. "I'll bake a few tuffs, as well," he shouted as they went out the door.

When they got back to the farm, Julie's mum and dad were there. Julie told them about the letter, and asked if they would ask Robert's parents to come to the carol service that night.

"Of course we will, dear," her mum replied. "Now, what can we do to help?"

"I think we are almost there," Sarah replied, "but if you want to come on down to the lodge, our guests should be arriving in about half an hour. I expect they will want a cup of tea, and we have all this shopping to put away down there."

When they got down to the lodge, Cart, Miss Pollard and Andrew were there. They came up to Julie. "The vicar wanted someone to say something about Christmas presents at the carol service tonight," Cart said, "so I suggested you. You're a good little talker."

"I don't know whether to take that as a compliment or not," she replied. "What can I say about presents, anyhow? Cart, why pick on me? You can go off people, you know." She had a big smile that said she really wanted to do it.

"Because we all loved what you said at the funeral. It all made a lot more sense than what the vicar says. You made people cry."

"That was then. That was words I meant. All my thoughts aren't like that. Anyway, I wouldn't like to make people cry at Christmas."

Andrew put his arm around her. "You are a girl that people have a lot of respect for," he said. "Now, you just say what you think and it will be fine."

Sarah asked Andrew if Jenny from the monastery was coming to the carol service. She thought it might be a good idea, as she would gradually get used to them, before Christmas day.

"Sister Louise and two of the nuns are coming. The two nuns are going to sing a duet. So I will ask them if they will bring her."

Julie's dad asked Andrew how he was involved with the monastery, as they were Catholic and he was Church of England.

"I take an interest in the community, whatever the religion. I think we can learn a lot from each other. It makes no difference to me if you are Baptist or Methodist; we are all human beings."

"I'm glad to hear that. It's so refreshing. The world would be a lot better if everyone in your position was the same.

That's the way we tried to bring our daughter up."

"And a credit she is to you. She must make you very proud."

Sarah shouted, "Our guests are coming." They all ran over to meet them.

Once the guests were all settled in, everyone but Sarah and Julie went home. They would all be back for the carol service.

The robin that seemed to follow Sarah everywhere was missing when they got back to the farm. It was funny; although no one spoke much about the robin each day, now they all missed her.

George came running in to the kitchen. "Robin," he shouted. He held his hand out and the robin was laying still on the palm of his hand. It took him quite some time for him to explain that the robin flew into the wall of the barn.

"Is she dead?" Sarah asked, as Fred took it from George.

"I'm not sure," Fred replied. He opened its beak and blew hard in to its mouth. The robin fluttered, and then suddenly it flew around the kitchen.

Julie and Sarah grasped hold of Fred and kissed him hard on each cheek.

"That's a Christmas present you could tell them about tonight," Sarah said to Julie. "Anyway, what are you going to say? Shouldn't you be writing something down?"

"You know me. I'm just going to say what comes into my head. But I still wish they hadn't asked me." But everyone knew deep down she was looking forward to it.

They all got ready and made their way down to the lodge for the service. Cart and Miss Pollard where already there. Cart had the fire going, both inside and out. It wasn't long before the villagers started to arrive and the service began. The whole valley echoed with the sound of carols.

The nun's duet was simply outstanding. Jenny, the girl

they brought with them, was very shy. But she soon started to talk to George. In fact, all the visitors seemed to get on with George.

You could tell George was pleased. It was the first time in his life he had met people like him.

Andrew said a short prayer. "Now, we all give and receive presents at Christmas, and Julie will now tell us about some."

Julie came out to the front. "Why would you want someone half most of your ages telling you about presents? I don't know what you like or what you want.

"What I do know is that we all have two big presents to give that don't cost a penny; they are, of course, love and forgiveness. I'm very lucky. I have great parents, friends and a boyfriend, and I love them all dearly, as I know they do me. I think the love bit is easy.

"But what about the forgiveness? That's hard. If someone calls you names in the heat of the moment, that's easy to forgive." She looked at Robert's mum and dad and smiled. "But if you call names with malice, then it is harder to be forgiving." She then turned and looked at Gilbert Lane as she continued. "If you are a tight old farmer that tried to fiddle a couple of young women out of a couple of pounds, then you can be forgiven. But if it means in doing so you are robbing people like this," she pointed to George and the guests, "then I'm sorry, there is no forgiveness. We all know what happened this year with Rupert Trelivan. I'm afraid that's another case of no forgiveness. Like being lucky in love, I'm also lucky in forgiveness, apart from what Rupert has done to my friends. I can forgive everything that has happened to me, and I am deeply in love, so I have the best Christmas present anyone could wish for. My big wish is that you can all say the same."

"Here, here," came a shout from the crowd. "Never have truer words been spoken."

Julie went over to where Sarah was standing. Sarah put her arm around her and whispered in her ear. "You could have told them a lot more about love. We all know you're the expert."

"There is love, and there is love," she replied.

With that, Gilbert Lane came around. "I've been trying to catch you two. I made a mistake adding up the other afternoon. I'm not sure exactly how much it should be, but five pounds should cover it." He passed Sarah a five-pound note.

"That's very honest of you," Sarah said. "Do you believe in forgiveness? I wonder if Miss Pollard will forgive you for pinching her bum," she laughed.

With that Miss Pollard came over. "Did I hear my name mentioned?" she said.

Sarah and Julie were giggling. Sarah said. "It was just Gilbert, saying he hopes you can forgive him."

Gilbert walked away. "It's like you say, dear; some things you can't forgive."

"How do you mean?" Julie said. "Surely someone pinching your bum is not all that bad?"

"Was that what he told you? I'm sorry, but I don't want to talk about it."

Julie could tell that they had upset her. She put her arm around her. "We are so sorry. We wouldn't have upset you for the world."

"That's all right, dears. You weren't to know. It all happened a long time ago. Now, let's just leave it at that."

Everyone had just finished singing the last carol. Andrew announced that there were pasties and mince pies inside the lodge and everyone was welcome. "I believe there is also some local cider and mulled apple juice," he said with a tone of excitement in his voice.

Everyone was mingling with one another. Fred was up at one end of the hall with all the visiting children. Children is probably not the right word, as some of them were older than Fred. But I think the oldest had the mind of a ten-year-old, which added to their charm. George and Jenny were also with them. Fred was making shapes with his hands, and the shadows were appearing on the large white wall that had just been painted. It was hard to believe that these people had never seen this before or even done it themselves.

George left the group for a minute and went over to Julie and pulled her arm. "What is it, George?" she asked.

"Name, name," he said.

"Whose name? I don't understand, you want to know a name?"

"No, Fred's name. They want Fred's name. What to call," George said. He was getting anxious.

Julie looked at him with a big smile. "They want to know what to call Fred, is that it?"

George nodded.

"Why not, "Uncle Fred"? Would you like me to tell them, or will you?"

George caught hold her hand and pulled her over to where they were all gathered.

"Hi, everyone," she shouted, "are you all having a good time? I'm Aunty Julie, and this is Uncle Fred. Now you all say after me, "Uncle Fred"."

Fred got Julie to stand so that her shadow was on the wall. He stood behind her and made shapes with his hands that made the shadow look like she had big ears. This brought much laughter to them all.

Jenny was so much like George. She had a plump face and a smile that would light a million glow-worms. She came over and put her arm around Julie. "I like you, Aunty Julie," she said, with that radiant smile.

Julie's smile was almost as big. "I like you, too," she replied.

Suddenly there was a large bang on the table. Everyone looked around; Cart was banging a spoon. "If I could just have your attention for a moment, and those of you who haven't got a glass of something would like to get one, because in a minute I'm going to propose a toast. But first, I would like to say a few words, which I don't do very often. You all might have heard how a group of youngsters ran riot in Tavistock last Saturday. Windows were smashed and there was a massive fight in the square. The headline of the local paper says "Typical Youth of Today". Now, I don't know many what they call youths, but there are four in this room that I have come to know well, and if there were ever four people that could be an example to the youth of today, it is those four. They could set an example to a lot of us old folk as well. Now, if I could just ask them to come over here a minute."

The four of them walked, embarrassed, across to Cart. "Now I'm going to ask you to raise your glasses to the four of them."

Everyone raised a glass. The four of them rang around the room.

John was the one that replied. "I don't think we are any different than most people of our age. I expect there were a few boisterous people around when you were young. I really just wanted to thank you all for coming tonight. I would also like to raise a toast to someone who, in a very short time, has become a very good friend. When he came over to see us for the first time, he took a shine to George. As time went on he began to think how lucky George was, having big open spaces to play in, animals that befriended him, and above all, villagers that took him to their heart. I can remember him saying to me one night, "I wonder how many people in George's predicament could walk to their village without being teased or snide remarks being made from every corner.""

"He then set out with a dream to help people who were less fortunate than George, even if it just relieved the parents for a while. Anyhow, without that dream,

this would never of happened. So please raise your glasses to a very dear friend, Fred."

The whole of the room raised glasses. "Fred," echoed in perfect harmony.

"Just, before you all go," Sarah shouted, "I know we will see a lot of you on Christmas day, but would anyone be interested in coming down on New Year's Eve for a cider and pasty evening?" Every hand in the room went up. "I'll take that as a yes then, so you better all come."

As they all left, Jenny came over to Julie. George was catching hold her hand. "Can I come again, Aunty Julie?" she asked. It was just like a child would ask.

"Of course, you can. We will see you on Christmas day," Julie replied. I'm sure there was a tear in her eye.

"Does Father Christmas come here?" she asked. George nodded, "He brought me a pig," he said.

Everyone left except Cart and Miss Pollard, who stayed and helped clear up.

They all walked up the lane together. "You will all have a busy day tomorrow," Miss Pollard said. "We will be over and give you a hand. What time would you like us to come?"

"The pair of you are so kind. I bet you pair were a credit to your generation," Julie said with a smile.

"I don't know about that. If I remember rightly, you were a bit of a bugger, Cart."

"Why, Miss Pollard, I'm surprised at you using a word like that. Anyway, I can't remember you being an angel," Cart replied.

"Perhaps it's a good job we have got to the end of the lane," John said with a hearty laugh. "I'll get the car and run you home."

"No, the walk will do us good," Miss Pollard replied. "Now, what time tomorrow?"

Sarah gave them both a kiss on the cheek. "Just come over when you like, but please don't go out of your way."

George had run ahead. Even though it was obvious he was tired out, he couldn't go to bed without seeing the owl.

Much of the next day (Christmas Eve) was spent getting ready for Christmas Day. Julie's dad had drawn the short straw; he was peeling all the potatoes. Her mum was preparing the veg. Sarah and Julie had gone in to Tavistock to do some last-minute shopping. Sarah wanted to buy all the guests that were staying a present. Fred was looking after the visiting children, although he only had to follow them around, as George seemed to have everything under control. He took them up to see the owl, over to the pigs, down to see the cows and calves. They went all the way up to Julie's Meadow, where the sheep were grazing. Fred stood back when they got to the pool, and George got them all to stand by the edge. "Angel," he said, pointing into the water. There was nothing there, but he remembered what people had seen.

The rest of the day flew by. It seemed no time at all before everyone was going home and the five of them were in the farm having supper.

Christmas morning had arrived, and everyone was excited. Sarah and Julie had gone down to the lodge to get the breakfasts. Fred, John, and George were going to have breakfast down there with the guests.

After they had had their breakfast, they had to get right on with dinner.

"I know this is a bit inconvenient," Fred said, "but could you spare Julie for half an hour?"

"Depends why," Sarah replied with a smile.

"All will be revealed, if it's a yes."

"Of course, it's a yes. Do we get to know what it's about now?" Sarah was sounding inquisitive.

"Afraid not. You will have to wait until we get back," Fred said with a nervous smile.

They made their way up to Julie's Meadow. "What are we doing up here?" Julie asked. 'Do you want to check the hay on Christmas morning?' She laughed out loud as she said it. "Might be a bit cold for me to take my knickers off."

"You can keep your knickers on. That's not what I brought you up here for."

They got to the pool. "This is where you first took advantage of me," he said, laughing.

"You didn't need any encouragement, if my memory serves me right. Now, come on, why have you brought me here?"

Fred took a big gulp. "When I was ten, my Nan was taken seriously ill."

"I remember, you were so upset. She gave you her ring, and you brought it over to show me. It looked beautiful to me then. Have you still got it?"

He took the ring from his pocket. "She told me I would meet someone special one day. Little did I know then that I had already met her." He gently took her hand and placed the ring on her finger. It fit perfectly. "Will you to marry me?" he asked.

She put her arms around him and squeezed as tight as she could. "I love you, Freddy kindness, I love you, I love you, I love you."

"Can I take that as a yes, then?"

"A thousand yeses! This is the best Christmas present anyone could ever wish for. Can I keep it on?"

"Of course, you can."

"I wanted to do it before, but I thought it would be nice on Christmas day. Now come on, we have to get back and help."

"Oh, really? I want to take my knickers off now. I suddenly feel quite warm."

"I'd like to take them off, but we do have to get back."

They ran all the way back. Julie was singing and skipping all the way. She ran into the kitchen down at the lodge where Sarah was lifting a pan of potatoes onto the stove. Miss Pollard was also there. She ran right up to them dangling her finger in front of her eyes.

"Is that what I think it is?" Miss Pollard asked.

"Oh, yes," Julie replied with a bit of swagger.

"That's wonderful!" Sarah exclaimed. "Come here and give me a hug."

"I'll have one of those as well," Miss Pollard said as she put her arms around her. "I think it's wonderful. I know you will be very happy."

"Have you seen my mum?" Julie asked with excitement in her voice.

"She is up at the farm, making some desserts in case someone doesn't like Christmas pudding." Sarah started to tease her, "You haven't got time to go up there now, we need you here."

"Oh, really it won't take me long. I would like to tell them."

"What do you think, Miss Pollard, shall we let her?" Sarah turned around to Miss Pollard, who was crying. "Why, Miss Pollard, whatever is the matter?" Sarah put her arms around her. She looked at Julie. "You run up and see your mum. We'll be all right."

Miss Pollard took a hanky from her pocket and dried her eyes. "Don't take any notice of me, dear. I'm just a bit down and excited for her."

"You've been doing too much for us, and we have been selfish and let you do it. Now come on, sit down and I'll make a cup of tea. I think we both deserve one."

"You haven't been selfish. Far from it. And I've loved every minute of it. I hope you will let me help for a long time to come."

Julie's mum and dad where delighted. Julie ran back down to help with the dinner. As people started to arrive, she held her hand out in front of them, and if they didn't notice, she held it closer to their face.

The dinner was a great success. After they had eaten and pulled their crackers, the place was full of chitchat and laughter. Then Father Christmas arrived with a present for all the guests that were staying, including the parents. George and Jenny were not left out. The way the visiting children reacted would bring tears to your eyes; it was obvious that they had never had anything like this before. Fred said just seeing the joy on their faces made it all worthwhile.

The afternoon had soon passed. It was just beginning to get dark. Cart had gone to get out of his Father Christmas suit, and John came in with the two large trays of mince pies that the baker had given them. "He said he had the oven on to cook the turkeys, so he rustled up a few mince pies."

Sarah and Julie were making tea and coffee. Fred was dishing out mulled wine. And John was handing out mince pies, with George and Jenny following with the clotted cream.

Sarah suddenly noticed Miss Pollard was missing. "Perhaps she went with Cart when he went to get changed."

"I don't think so. Cart was on his own. I do hope she is all right," Sarah said. "She seemed very down this morning."

With that, Cart walked back in. Julie beckoned him over and asked if he had seen her. "No," he replied, "but she has been acting strange all day. Don't worry, she will be back in a minute."

All the villagers had gone home. George wanted to take the other children up to see the owl. Fred said he would go with them.

Miss Pollard still had not returned. "Do you think she has gone back to her cottage?" Julie was trying to think positively.

"I wouldn't think so. I have the keys," Cart replied.

"We will have to go and look for her in case she has fallen down or something." Sarah was really getting worried. "Any idea where she might have gone?" she asked Cart.

"I don't know, sometimes lately she has been going up to Julie's Meadow, but I don't think she would go up there in the dark."

Julie grabbed her coat. "I'm going to see," she said as she ran out of the door.

When she got up to the gate of Julie's Meadow, she could a shape sitting down by the pool. She could soon see it was Miss Pollard. She went over and sat down beside her. "We were all worried about you," she said.

"Don't worry about me. I'm all right," she said, wiping a tear from her eyes.

"You aren't," Julie said as she put her arm around her.

"Do you think I'm an old fuddy-duddy? Do you know I'm only fifty-seven?" She started to cry.

"What's brought all this on? I don't think you are a fuddy-duddy. I see you as a lovely, caring person. Anyone can see how much love you have for people."

"Love: that's a word with many meanings. I can't give the love I want to give."

"How do you mean?" Julie couldn't understand what was the matter.

"You know, proper love with a man."

"Do you mean what I think you mean?"

"Yes, that's what I mean. I have never felt like this. If only it wasn't for my past."

"How do you mean? It doesn't matter about your past. Whatever it was, it couldn't have been that bad."

"Believe me, it was."

"Why don't you tell me. You never know, it might help."

"I have never told anyone. Everyone thinks of me as old Miss Pollard, with emphasis on the Miss. Why can't they call me Olive? They call everyone else by their Christian name."

"I don't know what to say. We all call you Miss Pollard out of respect for you."

"Respect. I lost that years ago. That's where it all went wrong."

"Why don't you tell me about it? I'm a good listener."

"Would you be shocked if I told you I was raped?"

"Yes, I would be. I know it must be hard, but it shouldn't alter you as a person."

"That's easy to say. I was a bit of a flirt, you know. I let this person feel my breasts, and I teased him a bit, I suppose. But when I left him, he followed me, and when I walked through the park, he pounced on me, forced me to the ground and forced himself on me."

"God, that must have been awful."

"The thing is, that wasn't the worst of it. I thought I was pregnant. I couldn't tell anyone, so I went to our local doctor. You had to pay back then. I had no money, but he said he would get rid of it. He was terrible. He made me do things to him, disgusting things. My body still creeps thinking about it. If I didn't do what he said, he would tell my mother. Five times I went back. He kept telling me the time wasn't right. The last time, he put his hands inside me so hard that it made me bleed. It really hurt. He told me I had to go back one more time, but I didn't. If only I had known I wasn't pregnant."

"How awful." Julie had started to cry. "However did you cope?"

"Lady Trelivan became pregnant, and I went away with her until Lord Trelivan came home. And that was that, really, but I have never been with a man since that day."

"Did you tell anyone?"

"Lady Trelivan knew, but no one else. And that's how I want it to stay."

"Your secret is safe with me, but don't you think if you talked to someone properly it might help? We all thought you and Cart, well, you know, were lovers."

"That's the problem. We sleep in separate rooms. I do so much want it to be more, but I'm afraid."

"Look, I can't begin to imagine what you are going through, and I'm certainly no expert. But I do know it's not all about sex. Yes, I do enjoy that, but sometimes, if I just snuggle up to Fred, we get just as much pleasure. Why don't you start with that and see where it goes?"

"That's all very well for you, but I wouldn't know how to approach the situation."

"You have to follow my instructions. This is my special remedy for Olive. Tonight, when you go to bed, wait for a while, then go into his room and say you are frightened and ask if you could stay with him."

Olive laughed, "What would I be frightened of?"

"You could say you thought you had heard a noise or something."

Olive started to laugh. "Oh, I don't know. That doesn't sound like me."

"We are talking about the new you. Now come on, we must get back. People are worried about you. But you must promise me you will do what I say. And I shall want a progress report."

"I don't want anyone to know about this, mind."

"We can say you just went for a little walk and fell down and had to rest awhile."

"This feels like the start of a new adventure. Thank you for listening. I feel so much better. Do you know what the

— 155

older boys down the school used to call me, because I'm a Spinster?"

"No."

"Come here, I will have to whisper it." Julie put her ear close to Olive. She whispered in it, "Leather fanny. Now what do you think of that?"

"Why, Olive, you have quite shocked me."

They approached the lodge. "Start to limp a bit," Julie said with a bit of a giggle.

"Is everything all right?" Sarah shouted as soon as they came into sight.

"Oh, its fine. Olive has had a bit of a tumble, but I think she's all right now." Julie had her arm around her as if to help her along. "Fred," she said, "would you be a dear and get the car to run her home?"

Fred ran up to the farm and got the car and ran Cart and Olive home.

When they were gone, Sister came to collect Jenny. "Can she stay?" George asked.

"We haven't got room," Sarah said, "but she can come over again, if it's all right with Sister."

George, with a big smile on his face, said, "She can share my room."

"I don't think Sister would go along with that," Sarah said, putting her arms around him.

When they got up to the farm, George and John went off to check the livestock. Sarah and Julie went into the kitchen. Sarah wanted to hear all about what happened to Miss Pollard. But Julie gave nothing away. "There is just one thing I found out. She wishes everyone would call her Olive."

That night, when Fred and Julie were cuddled up in bed, Julie suddenly turned around and put the light on.

"What's wrong?" Fred said with great concern in his voice.

"Oh, nothing," she replied. "I just haven't seen my ring for about an hour. I just want to make sure it's still there."

She turned to switch the light off. "No, leave it," he said, almost like an order.

She was kneeling on the bed, facing him. He slowly lifted her nightie, and removed it over her head.

"Am I dreaming, or is this really happening to us?" Fred knelt up in front of her. He put his arms around her. "Promise me I'm not going to wake up in a minute and you will be gone."

"That's one thing I can promise." Julie ran her hands up and down his back. "I can promise that because I love you, I love you, I love you, and I will always love you." She smiled and looked at her ring. "I love you nearly as much as my ring."

"That's all right, then. I love you nearly as much as …"

Julie put her hand over his mouth to stop him finishing the sentence. "You hadn't better love anything more than me."

He pulled the bed clothes back to the bottom of the bed. "Lie down," he whispered, "and let me show you how much I love you."

She lay down on the bed. He just looked at her for a few moments, taking in all her beauty.

It wasn't long before they were all cuddled up and fast asleep.

Over at Cart's cottage, it was a bit of a different story. Olive was lying in her bed, wanting to go into the next room with Cart. She was thinking of everything that Julie said, but couldn't bring herself to do it. She must have been there lying for three hours or more, when suddenly there was the sound of glass breaking. Cart woke up, startled, and jumped out of bed. He was bare-chested and had a pair of long johns on. As he got to the landing, he met Olive coming out of her room. "Did you hear that?" she gasped.

"Yes, I"ll go downstairs and check a minute. You wait here a moment," Cart said as he tiptoed down the stairs. "Nothing downstairs was amiss." He returned to Olive.

"Can I come in with you? I'm a bit frightened," she said, her heart thumping like Billy Brown's traction engine.

"Of course, you can. I'll sleep in the chair and you can have the bed."

"Oh, no need for that. I can sleep this side and face outwards, and you the other." She was feeling as excited as a child with a bag of sweets.

"If you are sure that's all right," he said, feeling quite pleased with the arrangement.

They got into bed, lying with their backs to each other. Olive was itching to turn around. She kept thinking if she didn't make a move now, she might never get another chance. With that, Cart turned and lay on his back. Her heart still pounding, she turned, put her arm across his stomach, nestled her head into his shoulder, and her head against his cheek, with a look of pure contentment on her face. Within minutes, they were both fast asleep.

Back at the farm, it was early rise, a quick cup of tea, and down to the lodge to get the breakfast going. Fred was going to take the guests to see the Boxing Day hunt assemble down at The Butcher's Arms. Sarah and John were out, then Fred came down. "Where's Julie?" Sarah asked.

"I'll go and wake her in a minute. I don't think she had a very good night. I think she was sleepwalking." Fred was sounding concerned about her.

"How do you mean?" Sarah could see the concern on Fred's face.

"I don't know. I woke up in the night put my hand out, and she wasn't there. The bed was quite cold, as if she had been gone for some time. With that she came in to the room and got into bed. I spoke, but she didn't answer. I'm sure she was asleep."

"I expect it's all the excitement," Sarah said as she went out the door to throw some bread out for the robin. As she turned to come back in, she noticed a pile of glass left on the seat outside the door. She picked it up and put it in the bin. She came back in. "I'll go on down and start the breakfast. I should let Julie sleep for a while. Just come on down when you are ready."

Sarah had just left when Julie came down. "Why didn't you wake me?" she shouted to Fred.

"I don't think you had a very good night."

"What do you mean? I had a wonderful night, didn't you?"

"Yes, but after, I think you went sleepwalking."

"Did I? Oh, well, it was still a wonderful night. Come on," she said, "we must hurry down and help Sarah."

As they went out the door, Julie turned to Fred. "Have you picked anything up from the seat?"

"No, like what?" he replied.

"Oh, nothing. I thought I left something there."

They had no sooner got to the lodge when Olive and Cart arrived. The both of them had a kind of glow about them.

Olive looked over to Julie and put her thumb in the air. "We just popped down to give you a hand before we have our breakfast."

"No, sit down," Sarah said, "I'll bring you over a cup of tea and we can all have breakfast together."

As they were drinking their tea, Cart said, "Funny thing happened last night. We were woken up by glass breaking. It sounded very close, but I can't find any anywhere."

"That's strange," Sarah said, "I found some glass …" Before she could finish what she was saying, Julie had brought her elbow into her ribs. "What did you do that for?" she exclaimed.

"Oh, I'm sorry. My arm just slipped. I hope it didn't hurt," Julie could hardly stop laughing as she said it.

They all sat and ate their breakfast. Julie and Sarah were going to stay and prepare the lunch for the guests, and clean the rooms while they were gone to watch the hounds.

"Why don't you go," Olive insisted to Sarah, "I can stay and help Julie, if she doesn't mind."

"No, I don't mind. It will do you good to get out for a bit."

As soon as they had gone, Julie sat Olive down. "Now, then," she said, "a quick cup of tea and a progress report."

"All went to plan, dear. It was like fate. No way could I have done what you said, but then suddenly some glass broke and that gave me the opportunity."

Julie caught hold her hand. "That's lovely. I'm so happy for you."

"Do you think I should try a snog tonight?" Olive said with a touch of laughter.

"I should. You have to strike when the iron's hot."

"Believe me, the iron was hot, all right, dear." I don't think anyone had ever heard Olive talk like that before.

"Why, Olive, I don't know what you mean." Julie was teasing her now.

"If ever the time arose, do you think I will know what to do? I think you can get a book down the library." Olive was thinking seriously.

"You won't need a book. Just flow with the tide, and everything will be fine." I think Julie was as excited as Olive.

Olive stood up. "All this chit-chat! We had better get on with the work." As they made their way to the guest's rooms, she put her arm around Julie. "I'm glad we had that chat yesterday," she said. "What a Christmas present, being turned into a new woman."

"We both had great Christmas presents," Julie said, flashing her ring in front of Olive. "You might get one next year," she said, laughing out loud.

The next few days passed away without too much ado. George and Fred had spent all their time with the visiting children, Olive and Cart were still sharing the same bed; whether it was still just cuddles, who knows, but the look on Olive's face would suggest things had progressed.

Sarah and Julie were spending their time planning the New Year's Eve party.

Nearly the entire village turned out for the party. John went and picked Jenny up from the monastery; Sister would collect her later.

The party was a great success. For Music they had the local folk group, Thistle and the Cornflowers, so-called as there was one man and five girls. It was soon clear that there was a bit more than folk music they could play and sing. They soon had the whole room rocking.

Everyone had noticed the change in Olive; to say she behaved twenty years younger would be an understatement.

The next day was full of mixed emotions; it was the day for the guests to go home, and they would be sorely missed, especially by George. It had been so good for him to have people he could relate to around.

# Chapter 4

With everyone gone, things had to get back to normal. There was farm work to do, work on how to move Trelivan Lodge forward, and who knows, perhaps a wedding to plan.

John said that with a busy time coming up, he wouldn't be able to spend a lot of time on the lodge, and Sarah would have her hands full as well.

"Why don't we ask Cart and Olive around? I think they want to be involved, if possible," Julie suggested.

"That's a good idea. I think you should ask Andrew, as well. You will probably need him to get the guests," Sarah said, "And even though John and I are busy, we will still be able to have some input."

"Let's have a meeting Saturday night. We can have a take-away," John suggested. He liked his take-away.

On that Saturday night, John and Fred came back with the take-away and they all sat around the kitchen table. It was quite strange. They had a lovely front room, but they never used it.

Andrew said that he had loads of inquiries from people wanting to stay.

The first thing they had to do was work out a price to stay. It was then decided that Julie should be employed full-time, and Olive part-time to help.

Once all this was out of the way, Andrew congratulated Julie on her engagement and asked if she had any wedding plans.

"I hope you will marry us. I want to get married in June, when all the flowers are out in the meadow, and I would like to get married up there."

Andrew decided to tease here. "I can't marry you, because you don't come to church."

"I go to my church, and that's where I want to get

married, so that must count." Julie was sounding a bit disappointed.

"Of course, I would love to marry you, but in all seriousness, I can't marry you up there. But you could get married in the church, and then we could have a blessing there."

"We will make sure you have the best wedding this village has ever seen," Olive pronounced.

"All I want is all my dear friends around me on that day." Julie was getting quite excited.

"That's my only regret," Sarah said, "I wish I had gotten married in church with my friends."

"Why don't you, then? We could have a double wedding. That would be all right, wouldn't it, Andrew?" Julie asked.

"Not really. In the eyes of the Lord, they are all ready married," Andrew replied.

"Yes, but I know a couple who retook their vows. Why can't they do that?" Julie so wanted this to happen. "Please, pretty please," she said, looking at him in a way that anyone would find hard to refuse.

"We could do a blessing, if that would service," Andrew replied.

"That's sorted, then. You and I are going down the aisle together." Julie was getting so excited.

"Hang on a minute, don't I have a say?" Sarah thought Julie was rushing things a bit. "It's your day, and us having a blessing might take it away from your day. And John might not want to do it, anyhow."

Julie immediately turned to John. "Tell her you want to. Go on, please."

John said, "Don't bring me into it. I will do whatever Sarah wants. I think it would be nice, but the decision has to be Sarah's."

"We can think about it. No rash decisions." Sarah was beginning to warm to the idea.

Julie turned to Olive. "You think it would be a good idea, don't you?" she said, looking for support.

"It's not my decision, and it wouldn't be right for me to influence one way or the other."

"That's enough on the subject for tonight," Sarah announced, "we can discuss it when I've had time to think."

Andrew announced he had to go and write his sermon and got up to leave.

"Do you think Sister would let me pick Jenny up tomorrow? I think it does George good to have a bit of company."

"I would think that would be ok. I could pick her up, as I have to go over first thing," Andrew said, "if you could take her back."

As everyone was leaving, Julie whispered in Olive's ear, "You haven't given me a progress report."

She whispered back, "Things are going well."

The next morning, John was going to collect a new bull from a farmer over Launceston way. Fred was going to spend the day with George and Jenny. Sarah and Julie decided to go to church.

On their way to church, they passed Cart's place. Olive was coming out of the gate. "Where are you pair off to?" she asked.

"We thought we would give church a try this morning," Sarah replied.

"That's good. We can walk together," Olive said as she got between the pair of them and locked arms with them.

Olive was really jovial. Sarah was laughing. "Who is this lady? Is she new to the village?"

Julie was wondering if last night was the night.

"This is the new me," Olive announced. "From now on I'm one of the girls."

"We are pleased to have you," Julie replied.

"Have you any more thought on the wedding," Olive asked Julie as they were walking along the road.

"We can't do anything until madam makes up her mind what she is doing."

Sarah said, "I know what I want to do, but no way am I going to take over your day."

"Why can't you see it would make my day if you would share it with me? We are best friends. We should share everything."

"That's all right. I'll have Fred tonight."

"I don't mean share quite everything. Fred's all mine and not for sharing."

"You still haven't answered my question," Olive said. "Is it a yes or no?"

"Of course, it's a yes."

Olive put her arms around them and turned them into a circle and they danced round and round like three four-year-olds.

After church, they told Andrew what they had decided. "That's fine. We will have to sort some dates out. It wouldn't do to take bookings for the lodge that week."

"You coming back for coffee?" Sarah asked Olive. "Good idea. Cart has gone over to Sid Rogers's. They plant their prize onion seeds now."

When they got back to the farm, John had arrived with the new bull. Fred, George and Jenny were watching him unload it. It certainly was a beautiful beast.

"We are going in for coffee. You going to join us?" Sarah asked.

"I'll just let the bull into the back yard a minute. I'll leave the halter on him for a while, so he gets a bit used to it."

"I better stay with George and Jenny," Fred said.

"Come on in and have a cup of coffee," Sarah insisted "They won't get hurt. George will look after her."

Coffee lasted for quite some time, with all the excitement of wedding plans. "You can be maiden of honour for both of us," Julie said, giving Olive a kiss on the check.

"Can I have someone to give me away?" Sarah asked. "I do hope so, because I would like Cart to do it. Do you think he would Olive?"

"I think he would be delighted; it's something we will have to ask Andrew."

"I hope I can still have John for best man," Fred did manage to get a word in.

"I don't see why not, dear." Olive's voice was so full of excitement. "Look at the time," she said. "Cart will be back for something to eat. I must fly."

"I better go and put the bull up with the cows," John said.

"Shall we go with him?" Julie suggested.

"You just want to see if the bull can give you any new ideas," Sarah said as she put her coat on with a giggle.

The pair of them giggled like a pair of excited children.

When they got out in the yard, the bull was nowhere to be seen, nor were George and Jenny. They shouted and searched all the buildings, but to no avail. John suggested that they might have gone down to the lodge. They searched down there. No luck.

Sarah didn't think George would go out in the road.

"I don't know," Fred said, "if the bull got out, he might have gone after him."

"I think we should look up across the fields, because if I was a bull, that's where I would go." Trust Julie to think logically.

They scampered up across the fields. When they started to cross Julie's Meadow, they could see, there by the pool, sitting on the ground, were George and Jenny. They were catching hold hands, and in their hands they had the Bull's halter. The bull was standing up behind them with its head over the top of theirs.

*— 166 —*

"That's so beautiful. Let's just sit here for a minute and let them have a bit of time," Julie said.

It brought a tear to Sarah's eyes as she said, "I wish I had a camera. It would make a picture that would adorn a million homes."

Fred looked at John. "It's a good job you bought a quiet bull."

"That's the point. We had a job to get him in the trailer. He was quite wild."

With that they got up. "Let's hide and watch them." Julie just wanted to see what was coming next.

They lay flat on the ground so that they couldn't be seen. George and Jenny walked on up across the meadow, still going away from the farm.

George had hold of her hand, and with the other hand he led the bull.

Julie and gang followed them all the way up and around the old quarry, back down the old lane and down to the lodge. There they sat again for about ten minutes. Then they got up and made their way up to the farm. When they got there, they just sat on the barn steps with the bull beside them.

They had no idea that they had been followed when John approached them. "Do you think I can have my bull back now?" he laughed. "Would you like to take him up to the cows?"

George just smiled. He caught hold Jenny's hand, and again with the other hand he led the bull. This time they had to go down through the village, and up the back lane to the field were the cows are.

As they passed Cart's house, Julie ran in to get Olive to see. Both Olive and Cart joined them.

"You know, people say good memories stay with you always; I think this is one that will last forever." Julie was now sounding emotional.

When they got back to the farm, Sarah realised that they hadn't had any dinner. "That's a letdown," John said jokingly. "No Sunday roast."

"No Sunday roast could ever compare to what we have just witnessed," Julie said. She would forgo a million roasts just to see what they had seen.

She turned to Sarah with a big grin on her face. "Shall I get some tiddies out of the bag and do some chips?"

This had become a bit of a joke. "Yes, you get the tiddies and John will peel them, since it's his belly that's asking."

"I don't know how to peel tiddies. You will have to show me, Julie."

"Be quicker if I peel the buggers myself."

"That's the answer I wanted to hear," he replied.

That night in bed Julie, cuddled into Fred as close as she could. "I'm in a snuggle mood tonight," she said. "Happy days like today make me all snug-a-lee and contented."

"Me, too," he replied as he put his arm around her and hugged her tight.

The next morning around about lunch time, Mr Knight the solicitor came around. "Nice to see you," Sarah said. "I hope this is a social call, and nothing is wrong."

"Bit of both, dear," he replied. "You will hear from the police, but I thought I would come around and let you know that the date for Rupert Trelivan's trial is the ninth of February."

"That's quick," Sarah replied. "I thought these things took ages."

"All depends on how busy the courts are, and whether the prosecution has its case ready," he replied.

"It will just be a formality, won't it?" Julie asked.

"I'm not sure; it is believed he is going to plead not guilty."

"How can he?" Julie was getting mad. "He admitted it. He has to go to jail and stay there."

"I don't care one way or another." Sarah was sounding quite philosophical. "What will be, will be."

"How can you say that? He killed your mother and baby." Julie was now madder than ever. "How could you ever forgive him?"

"Oh, I can never forgive him, and of course I hope he gets is comeuppance, but what difference will it make to me if he gets one year or twenty years? I'm having the best time anyone could ever wish for, and don't want anything to change it."

Julie put her arms around her. "God, you are a remarkable person," she said. "I wish I could be like you."

"Don't you ever change," Sarah replied. "If anyone is remarkable, it's you, not me."

"Will any of us have to go?" John asked.

"It depends. Chances are some of you, if not all of you, could be called as witnesses."

"I hope not. I don't want to go through it all again. I just want to get on with my life." Sarah just wanted to put the past behind her.

Mr Knight caught hold of Julie's hand. "I hear congratulations are in order. Have you set a date yet?"

"Not yet, other than that it will be in June."

"Lovely month, June," he replied. "All the flowers are out."

"Did you know Sarah is being blessed the same day?"

"I think that's lovely. I'm a proper old romantic at heart, you know."

After Mr Knight had left, Julie suggested they go and see Andrew to see what dates where available.

"You have only been engaged five minutes. Fred might not want it to happen so quick." Sarah thought Fred might want a say in the proceedings.

"You know me. As far as I'm concerned, it's Julie's day, and I will go along with whatever she wants."

Sarah looked at Julie. "I shouldn't get married, because that will all change then."

"Don't you believe it," Julie replied. "He knows what side his butter's spread on."

Sarah roared with laughter. "Don't you mean bread?" she asked.

"Bread, butter; what's the difference, as long as Fred knows who's boss," Julie replied, joining in the laughter.

John told Sarah, "She had better go and see Andrew, as we won't get any peace until the date is fixed."

Fred joined in. "Do you think we will get any peace then?"

"That's it. I've gone of the lot of you. I think I will run away with George." she turned to George "That will be all right, won't it?"

Poor George didn't know they were joking. He started cry. "Fred," he said, catching hold of Julie's hand. He led her across the room; he caught hold of Fred's hand and put it in Julie's. "Kiss, kiss," he said.

Julie looked up and gave Fred one big kiss.

"They're best friends," George said as he too started to laugh.

"Come here." Julie turned to George. "I want to give you a cuddle, I can love you as well."

He put his arms around her with a big beaming smile on his face. "Love Julie," he said.

That evening, Sarah and Julie went down to see Andrew to discuss the wedding. They weren't there that long; Andrew said he would need to spend some time with them, closer to the time, to discuss the bells, etc. But the main thing now was to fix the date, and they all agreed on June the eighth.

Andrew suggested that they not take any bookings for the lodge for the week before or the week after. "Give you a bit of time to enjoy it all."

As they were walking back, they meet John, George and Fred walking down the road. "And where do you think you are off to?" Sarah asked.

"We couldn't bare the suspense, so we thought we would come and meet you, since it's such a lovely night."

Julie couldn't wait to tell them the date. She just blurted out, "June the eighth, bells and everything."

The evening was very mild for January. The moon was shining so bright it was almost like daylight. "It's so beautiful. Shall we go for a walk?" Julie suggested.

"You can." Sarah replied, "but I've done enough walking for one day."

"I'll come with you," Fred said, "as long as we don't go too far."

Fred and Julie made their way up the back lane. The other three returned to the farm. They went in the gate to the field where the bull and cows were. The cows looked wonderful; their deep, red colour with the orange moon shining made them glow like fire.

They walked up across the field to their shed. "Let's just sit here for a while," Julie said.

They opened the doors wide and sat on the hay, looking out of the door, with their arms around each other in complete silence. Everything looked so magical.

"What are you thinking?" Fred asked Julie.

"I was just looking over at the woods. It was as if Pooh Bear could appear at any moment. I can just imagine him carrying his honey pot and honey dipper. What are you thinking?"

"Oh, I'm just thinking how lucky I am. If what I can see is only a fraction of the world, I don't want to see any more. This is more than sufficient for any man."

She turned and kissed him. "I do love you," she said.

Fred put his hands down and started to undo her dress.

"What, may I ask, are you doing?" she asked rather excitedly.

"Actually, I'm Pooh Bear, and I'm looking for my honey pot," he replied.

"Do you think you will find it down there?"

"Trust me, I know I will," he said as he reached the bottom button.

"If you want any clues, I think you are quite warm." And with her hands wandering, she whispered, "I think I have found the honey dipper."

It was nearly two hours before they returned to the farm. You can guess what Sarah's comments were.

Things were running along quite smoothly over the next few weeks; the lodge was full every week, and Jenny was coming over every weekend. John had got the local builders in to do up the house down by the lodge. He asked Sarah if she would help him out, as she was down there each day. She could be in charge of how to lay out the kitchen and what colour the rooms should be painted.

It was only a week until the trial. John and Fred had been summoned as witnesses. It was all a bit scary.

It was late in the afternoon when Cart came driving down the lane. Everyone looked in amazement; he was on what looked like a train, and Olive was sitting on the back. "What you think?" he said.

"Bloody brilliant," Fred replied. "Where did you get it?"

"I made it for you to take the guests around on."

"It's been a big secret," Olive said. "He didn't let me see it until today."

"How did you make it?" Julie asked in amazement.

"I don't know how much I should say really. You see, I built it around a T-20 tractor. The only problem is, I don't know who the tractor belongs to. The estate brought it down for me to do some welding over a year ago. No one ever came back for it. As there is no estate as such now, I thought I would put it to good use."

"You have certainly done that. Can we all go for a ride now?" Julie asked like an excited school girl.

"Come on, Fred. I'll show you the controls. The rest of you jump on."

Julie gave Cart a big kiss on the cheek as she passed.

They took the train up the lane into the farmyard, up across the fields, through Julie's Meadow, up around the top of the quarry, back down the old lane and back to the lodge.

"Do you think your guests will like it?" Cart asked.

"Like it? I think they will love it. I just don't know what to say." Fred was completely overwhelmed.

"Do you mind if I come up and take them out sometimes? I like to drive it; something about driving something you have made."

"Be glad for you to. You know you are more than welcome anytime," Fred liked having Cart around.

"I think it should have a name," Sarah said, tapping the bonnet as if it was human.

John thought they should all go down the pub and toast her. They could also choose a name.

Sarah said she thought the train should be called Angel, after the man that made her.

"Bugger me, I'm no angel," Cart replied.

"You are to us," Julie said, "and I think the name is appropriate."

"You girls know how to make a man feel proud," Cart said, "I only do what I enjoy doing."

"Is that right, Olive?" Julie asked, "And what does he like?"

"Oh, this and that." Olive's face went red. "Now, let me buy you all a drink," she said, changing the subject.

With the name of the train agreed upon, the conversation turned to the trial. Sarah suggested that she speak to

Mr Knight for a bit more advice. She was adamant that she didn't want to attend.

On the Friday before the trial, Mr Knight came around to discuss how he could help. "I shall be attending every day, not in a professional capacity, but as a friend," he said. "I can come around and give you an update each night if you like."

Sarah said that would be much appreciated.

On the day of the trial, everyone was bit edgy. John and Fred had gone to the assizes. Julie and Sarah had to entertain the guests, with the help of George and Olive.

The big black and white sow had just farrowed again, and the baby piglets were of great interest to the guests. This made the day pass quite quickly.

John and Fred returned home just after lunch. They were told they wouldn't be called that day.

Later on, Mr Knight arrived. "How it is going?" Sarah asked.

"Not too good. He's pleaded not guilty to all the charges. The day has been taken up with legal arguments. It doesn't look like the judge will allow the statements from John and Fred. I'm not sure what the problem is, but it would appear the police have dropped a boo-boo somewhere along the way."

"What does that mean?" Julie asked.

"Well, without their evidence of what Rupert told them, I'm not sure what other evidence they have. We will have to see how tomorrow goes."

The next day, Fred and John were again sent home. They were told that they could not enter the public gallery, as they might still be called, but at the moment it was unlikely.

When Mr Knight came around, he explained that the judge ruled their evidence inadmissible. "The police have said that it was their intention to arrest Rupert at the hotel. But they let him come into the room with John and Fred with a police officer present before they arrested him.

"The problem is, the officer in the room has logged the time at eleven thirty-five, which is probably right.

"But the arrest is logged at ten thirty, and the caution at fourteen hundred hours. Now, it would seem that there is a mistake in the arrest time."

"What difference does that make?" Sarah asked.

"Well, the defence argued that if the time of the arrest was right, then Rupert should have been cautioned then. This means anything said between the time the arrest was logged and the time the caution was logged can't be used in evidence.

"And it would appear that the judge agreed. He thought there was too much doubt, and he would not allow the evidence, or any mention of it to the jury."

John thought it a bit harsh, as it was pretty obvious it was just a mistake.

Mr Knight explained, "That's the way the law works. That's why it is essential that you get everything right before you get to court."

"Does it make much difference? They still have the car, and it is pretty obvious he tied his mother up. Plus there is that Rosemary women who pretended to be his mother. Surely any jury would find him guilty." John was thinking quite positively.

"Well, we just have to see how things go tomorrow," Mr Knight said as he bid them good night.

The following day, John and Fred were sent home again, and this time they were told they did not have to come back unless they were sent for.

When they got back to the lodge, no one could be found. After a few minutes, they realised that the train was missing. "Cart must have come over and taken them all out," John said.

"If we walk up the lane, we can meet them. I expect they have taken the same route." Fred was a little anxious.

They walked up the old lane, around by the quarry and back down via Julie's Meadow, but they were nowhere to be seen.

"I wonder if they are down at Cart's," John thought. "I can't think anywhere else they could be."

As they were walking down the road, they meet Julie walking up the road. "I think we have run out of diesel," she shouted.

John asked where they had been.

"Up on Dartmoor," she replied.

"Dartmoor," John said with the tone of astonishment in his voice. "What was Cart thinking about going all that way?"

"Oh, Cart's not with us," Julie replied.

"Then who's driving?" Fred asked.

"Sarah. Good driver she is, too. Now, we better get back to them with some diesel. Julie asked Fred if he would run her back in the car.

When they got back to the train, PC Roberts was there with his notebook out. Julie ran up to him. "Everything all right?" she asked.

"Not really. I can't find a tax disc," PC Roberts replied.

"Trains don't have tax discs," she answered back jovially.

"This isn't a proper train though, is it?" PC Roberts had the voice of authority.

"If it's not a train, what is it?" Julie had her face right up to his, looking deep into his eyes.

PC Roberts had gone bright red. "Umm, I don't know," he said. He thought for a moment, then replied, "Trains run on rails, and there are no rails here."

"That's not our fault, then is it? If there were rails here, we could go on them. You better get on to the council and tell them we want some rails. Now, can we go," she said, pouring the diesel into the tank.

"Yes, on your way. And I will see what the council has to say."

They got back to the lodge. Sarah and Julie thought it was a big joke what they had done, but John was furious. He didn't say anything in front of the guests, but he certainly let them know when they were on their own.

Sarah whispered to Julie, "We better watch to see where he hides the keys."

Mr Knight arrived to give them a rundown on the day's proceedings. "Things aren't going too well. Rupert has been giving evidence to day.

"He said he did tie his mother up and put her in what he called a shed. He said he did intend to go and let her out. But when everyone said she had gone away, he thought she had got out and ran away.

"He was then asked about Rosemary. If he thought his mother was alive, why didn't he look for her, rather than get someone to take her place?

"He said that Rosemary approached him; he genuinely thought she was his mother.

"He did admit to taking the wages from the estate. He also admitted knocking down your mum. He said it was an accident."

"Accident, my ass," Julie said. "Do you think he is going to get away with it?"

"It's all up to the jury. I think the expert the police had might have convinced them that the damage to the car and the hairs found on it mean no way it could be an accident. We might know tomorrow. We have the summing up in the morning, and if the jury finds it easy to reach a verdict, we may get it tomorrow."

"I do hope so. Then we can all put it at the back of our mind and move on. I just want to remember my mum as she was, not what happened to her." Sarah had tears in her eyes.

"Come on," Julie said, "we can all celebrate when it's all over. You know, it's Valentine's Day on Saturday."

"I suppose you think we will have to take turns going up to the shed. Or do you want it all to yourself?" Sarah said with a big grin.

Julie said it wasn't safe for her to go up there anymore.

Sarah asked why not.

Julie got close to Sarah's ear and whispered, "Pooh Bear lives up there. I have seen him and his honey dipper."

Sarah didn't have a clue what she was talking about.

The next day, the five of them stayed close together. Very little work was done; their minds were on the trial.

"Good news," Mr Knight said on his arrival, "guilty on all counts. Because of his age when he killed his mother and the mitigating circumstances, the judge only committed him to three years. For the murder of your mother, which the Judge said was cold and calculated, the judge sentenced him to life. I think the jury could see right through him."

"That's all over with now," Julie said, suggesting they should all go out on Valentine's night for a meal.

"Good idea. I think we should ask Cart and Olive, and I wonder if Sister would let Jenny come?" Sarah was quite excited. She was glad it was all over.

You would never believe that George could possibly know what was going on, but when he went over to the barn, the owl and the robin where both there, and he told them word for word what Mr Knight had said. The robin just started to sing as if with delight.

It flew out of the barn, across the yard and into the kitchen.

"Look," Julie said excitedly, "see who has come to join the celebrations."

Sarah looked at the robin that had perched on the back

of one of the chairs. "It's all over now, my baby, it's all over," she said.

The robin lifted her head and started to sing. Both Sarah and Julie had tears in their eyes.

"I'm going over to see George," Fred said.

"Come on," Julie said, "we will all come with you."

When they got to the barn, George was nowhere to be seen, nor was the owl. "They must have gone up across the fields," Fred said, walking towards the gate.

They went up across the field towards where the cows were and there they were. George had his arms around the bull's neck, and the owl was on the bull's back. George was telling the bull everything.

They got over beside him. "I don't understand," Julie said. "If owl's your mum and robin your baby, who the hell is the bull?"

George turned around with a big grin. "Dad," he said. "It's Dad."

"God," Sarah said, "my dad." She put her arms around Julie. "This is going too far. If this carries on, we will be called the weirdoes at Tremarrow Farm."

Julie sat down on the ground and pulled Sarah down beside her. "Don't start disbelieving now. I think," she said, "that they come back when there is something to come back for. You must have been very special to them. They must have loved you a lot to come back."

"I loved my mum, and I was very fond of Lord Trelivan. If only I knew he was my father, I could have given so much more."

"Do you know, I think they are here as they don't want to miss your wedding. I don't think the bull will be able to come to the church though," Julie said with a laugh.

Julie had a bit of a plan; she wanted to keep a secret. The next day, she went to see Cart to see if he could help. She asked Cart if it was possible to get a bull to pull a cart.

"What's all this about? Yes, providing the bull is strong enough, and the cart's not too big."

Julie told him about the robin, the owl and the bull.

"I'm not sure I quite believe it. But I would like to think you're right."

"Anyhow, the bull won't be able to come to the wedding. Unless, that is, he takes Sarah in a cart. Now what do you think?"

"Come out the back a minute." The back of Cart's place was like Aladdin's cave. He pulled a tarpaulin off an old trap. "It needs a paint job, but what do you think?"

"Absolutely brilliant." She gave Cart a kiss on his cheek. "Not a word to Sarah, mind," she said as she skipped towards the gate.

When she got back to the farmyard, Sarah was leaning on the gate, looking at the pigs rolling in the mud. She looked deep in thought.

"Penny for them," Julie said as she approached.

"Oh, I was just thinking, if the robin is my baby, the owl my mum and the bull Dad, who are these dirty little buggers?"

Julie laughed. "You probably wouldn't want to know, but I bet they have a good life whilst they're here. Might be one of Gilbert Lane's relations," she laughed.

With that, the owl flew down and pitched on one of the little pigs backs. "There," Julie said, "your mum knows one."

"At least it's the cleanest one," Sarah replied. They both thought it extremely funny.

They both leaned on the gate and started to talk about wedding dresses. Sarah said she wouldn't be able to get married in white.

Julie said they should have the same colour. She didn't want a big white dress with a veil. "I just want a nice, smart suit or dress," she said.

Sarah thought they should go to Plymouth the following week and see if there was anything they liked.

"Could we take Olive with us?" Julie thought she would like to be involved.

"Of course, I would love to have her input. Do you know if I still have to have someone to give me away? I do hope so."

"You can have whatever you like; it's your day." Julie suddenly thought, "I better tell my parents. They wouldn't like it if they heard from someone else. Anyhow who would you have to give you away?"

"I would like Cart. He is a wonderful friend to us all."

"We have so much other stuff to sort out; it's only four months away." Julie was sounding excited.

That evening, Fred took Julie around to see their parents to tell them about the wedding.

Julie cuddled up close to Fred in the car on the way home. "I am so happy," she said, "I just love you to bits. Do you think Pooh Bear will come indoors tonight?"

"I expect so, but you know, bears are very unpredictable," Fred replied with a grin.

With her hands wandering, she said, "I hope he brings his honey dipper."

Fred laughed as he replied, "They say he never leaves home without it."

The next morning, Sarah was down helping Julie with the guests' breakfasts, when down came George with one of the pigs. He was really excited. "Mummy's friend," he said, "Mummy's friend."

Julie was deep in thought. "Do you know, I think George is blessed with something special." She turned to Sarah, "Can you think who this pig can be?"

"No," Sarah replied, "but I will ask Olive if she knows who it might be."

— *181* —

They were all quite excited on Valentine's Day. George had borrowed a tie from John, as he wanted to look his best. He was so proud of the way he looked, he went out to show the owl and the pig. The robin followed him over, chirping all the way.

George rode with Fred and Julie, as they were going to pick Jenny up, and Cart and Olive rode with John and Sarah.

Over the meal, the topic of the wedding came up. Olive thought it would be all right for someone to give Sarah away.

"I'm so glad." Sarah put her hands across the table, and she caught hold of Cart's hand. "And will you give me away?" she asked.

"Bugger me," he replied in astonishment. "I don't know what to say," wiping a tear from his eye. He took a deep breath. "I would bloody love to it; would be a great honour."

Olive, too, had tears in her eyes. "I think that's wonderful. What dear friends you are."

Sarah asked Olive if she knew anyone her mother was friendly with.

"Not really, dear, your mother was friendly with everyone."

"Can you think of anyone who would look for her?" Sarah really wanted to know.

George suddenly said, "Smoky."

"What is it?" Julie asked him, "Too smoky for you?"

"No, pig Smoky," he replied.

"That's it," Olive said, "Your mother's friend, Smoky Alice. She lived in the shed at the bottom of the lane. She always had a smoky fire burning and smelt of it. The villagers were afraid of her, but your mother had a lot of time for her. She knew more about her than she ever let on.

"That explains the pig," Julie said, "but how did George know who she was?"

"She used to come up to your mum's for meals when George was a baby. I do know your mum used to say she told great stories."

The next morning, George disappeared right after breakfast, soon to appear with the bull on a halter, the pig following behind, the owl on his shoulder, and the robin flying with them.

John ran in to get everyone out to see. They all thought it wonderful. John said he hoped there were no more reincarnations to come.

"I think it's wonderful," Sarah said, going over and giving George a kiss.

"I just hope the bull finds time to do what he is supposed to do."

John was standing right behind the bull, who suddenly broke wind. It was right on cue, and as if done on purpose.

"That told you, then," Julie said, roaring with laughter.

Sarah and Julie went on down to get the guests' breakfast. George followed with the animals; it was scenes like this that made this a truly magical place, and memories that would stay with the guests forever.

"Shall we have a look around the house and see how the builders are doing?" Sarah thought they should be there by now.

They went inside. The house was being done so beautifully; the views out of the windows were outstanding, and you could see the whole valley opening up in front of you.

"What are you going to do with it?" Julie asked.

"Oh, John has plans when it is finished."

Things went on as normal over the next few weeks. The four of them were in the kitchen discussing the wedding. "I think we should look for somewhere to live when we get married," Fred said, knowing Julie really wanted to stay where they were.

"Oh, there is no rush, surely. We love you here," Sarah said, then she changed the subject. "By the way, when is your birthday, Julie?"

"April the eighteenth, and Fred's is the nineteenth," she replied. "Why, do you think we should have a party?"

"I think that's a great idea." John was all for it. "How old are you?" he asked.

"The big two-O," she replied. "Do you think we can get Thistle and the Cornflowers to play?"

"That's a good idea. We can soon get a buffet up, pasties and cold meat and things." This was the child in Julie coming out.

When they told Olive and Cart about the party, Olive said, "How can there be such a wise head on so young shoulders?"

It was two days before the birthday party. Andrew came around to say that Sister from the convent had had a stroke. "I know it is a lot to ask, but do you think Jenny could come over by day for a while?"

Sarah immediately said, "Of course. Fred or John will pick her up."

"No need for that. I will pick her up, as I will go over most mornings to see how Sister is."

John had gone to Tavistock market to buy some more cows. When he returned he had bought two cows, and three geese.

"Why on earth have you bought geese?" Sarah asked.

"They were cheap, they will make a good meal and wonderful house guards."

The geese were just left to wander around the yard. "We will have to make sure they don't go down the lodge. They might frighten the guests," Sarah said. I think she was afraid of them.

It was the morning of the party. Sarah was out early. She

— *184* —

had arranged for Olive to come in early, so that they could get the guests" breakfast, and then Sarah could get back to the farmhouse to spend some time with Julie.

Fred and Julie came down to the kitchen, followed by John. The geese were making the most terrible noise. "I don't think that was one of your best buys," Fred said, putting his hand to his ears.

"To be perfectly honest, I didn't know I bid for them, but the auctioneer knocked them down to me. Don't tell Sarah. I can't stand the bloody things. I'm going to Hatherleigh market next week, so I'll sell them up there."

Julie ran on down to help Sarah, and it wasn't long before they were back at the farm in the kitchen. "You and Fred sit down," Sarah said to Julie, "you have to take it easy on your birthday."

"I'm twenty, not sixty, you know," Julie replied.

The next thing John came into the room with a big parcel. He looked at Fred. "I know your birthday is in a couple of days, but this is from Sarah and me, with all our love."

"That's a bit sentimental for you," Julie said, laughing. Her face was lit up with excitement. "Come here, Fred," she said, "we will open it together. They quickly took off the first layer of paper, then another, then another. The parcel was getting smaller and smaller. The excitement had gone from Julie's face. "Is there anything in here?" she asked. With that, a pile of papers fell on the ground. "What is it?" she said, looking rather bemused.

"Open them up and see," Sarah said. It was she who was excited now.

Fred opened up the papers and started to read them. "Is this what I think it is?" he said. "We can't possibly accept this."

"What? What is it?" Julie asked.

"It's the deed to the house down by the lodge," Fred explained.

"What, you mean we can rent it?" Julie said; the excitement had returned.

"No, not rent," Sarah said. "It's yours. We want to give it to you."

Julie sat down hard on a chair. "I don't know what to say. It's like Fred said, how can we accept it?"

"Of course, you can," John said. "I could give you a list of reasons why you can, but the main reason is we want you to have it, and that's all that matters, really."

Julie stood up and put her arms around him and gave him a big hug and a massive kiss.

Fred held his hand out. "I won't give you a kiss, but let me shake your hand."

Sarah beckoned Fred to her. "There is nothing stopping you giving me a kiss," she said, holding her arms out.

"When can we move in?" Julie asked. When Julie got excited, it was like the moon, the sun and the stars came together and lit up her face.

"Whenever you like," John said.

"We will have to get a bed," Julie shouted.

"Trust you to want the bed first," Sarah replied with a smile.

"Can we go down now? I'm so excited. It's my best birthday ever. Can I tell my mum and dad?" Julie looked at Sarah. "This is true? It is ours? It's not a joke?"

With that, Andrew arrived with Jenny. "How's the sick?" Fred asked.

"Not too good. I don't know what the outcome will be. It's Jenny I feel sorry for."

"Don't worry about Jenny. We will look after her," Sarah replied.

"That's fine short term. It's the long term I worry about." Andrew was so sincere.

Andrew left, and they all made their way down to the lodge.

George had gone up to the field and gotten the bull and – yes, you guessed it – the pig, the owl and robin came too.

When they got down to the lodge, Olive and Cart were decorating the hall for the party.

"Got something here for you two," Cart said, producing an envelope from his pocket. "Now I know the wedding is over a month away, but Olive and I thought we would give you a joint birthday and wedding present, now you are house owners."

"What, you knew all about it?" Julie said, giving Cart a hug and taking the envelope out of his hands the same time.

"Oh, yes," Olive laughed, "we knew all right. Sarah found it hard to keep it a secret."

Julie opened the envelope. It was a voucher to spend in Bartlett's furniture store. "Look!" Julie just burst in to tears.

Olive put her arm around her. "Come on, dear, whatever is the matter? We all thought you would be happy."

"Happy? I've never been so happy in my life," she sobbed. Still sobbing, she said, "why you are all being so kind to us?"

Sarah came over. "Come here and give me a cuddle," she said, laughing. "Promise me, if you are happy now, don't let me see you when you're sad. Now, why don't you and Fred go and look around the house?"

They went over to the house and looked around. "We will be happy here, won't we?" Julie asked Fred.

"Of course, we will. We would be happy anywhere as long as we had each other." He pulled her to him and gently kissed her on the lips.

"I'm glad, but something seemed to trouble you when we were outside."

"Oh, it's just Jenny. I worry what will happen to her if anything happens to Sister."

"I do have the solution. She could live with us; we could take care of her."

"That's not a decision to take lightly." Fred wanted to, but he didn't want Julie to do something she might regret later.

"Oh, I'm not taking it lightly. I don't care how hard it is. If she only had that smile once a month it would all be worthwhile." Julie really wanted it to happen.

"We will just see what happens. But if you really don't mind, it will put my mind at rest," he replied.

"It's no wonder I love you, Freddy kindness. Let's go and see how the party arrangements are going."

When they came over to the lodge, Olive, Cart, John and Sarah where sitting on the bench outside the lodge. John had his head in his hands. Sarah was laughing, George had the bull hold, the pig was there, the robin was on the pig's back, the owl was on George's shoulder, and Jenny had a goose with a piece of baler cord around its neck for a lead.

"Some guard goose that is," Fred shouted.

"Don't go there," John replied, "She's calling it "Mummy"."

"That's lovely," Julie said, "perhaps it is."

"You certainly started something with all this," John said to Julie. "Where is it all going to end? I've a bull that's supposed to sire the cows, but he hasn't got time because he is going walkies all day, I've a pig that I can never sell for bacon, now a goose that I don't like is going to be here forever. Could someone please tell me what's next? A lamb, a chicken? What, why me, why here?" He turned to Cart. "Do you believe they're someone?"

"It's a nice thought. I would like to think so, but find it hard to believe."

"I believe it anyway," Sarah said.

"Come with me," Julie said, "I'll show you something."

They all walked up to Julie's Meadow. They sat down in the middle of the field. There was a mist covering the valley below, the water in the large pool was glistening. Even though there were no flowers, the whole place had a magical feel.

"Now, I believe this is one of God's special places, not just because of the magic that's in the air, but of the love of the people that come here. Real love for other people. I believe God believes you are true Christians." Julie was preaching a bit of a sermon. "You might not go to church regularly, but God doesn't worry about that. Oh, yes, Fred and I sleep together and we're not married yet. God won't worry about that. What God does worry about is if he fails us when we are alive. And if he thinks he failed, he will make up for it when we die. That's how people are reincarnated, but not just anywhere. The place and time have to be right. This is certainly the right place, and I can't think of a better time."

"I would love to think you are right," John said, "but what would have happened if I hadn't bought the bull or the geese?"

"Oh, I think God had a hand in that. It was probably him that was bidding, not you," Julie said with a smile.

Sarah caught hold of Julie's hand. "I know what I believe. My mum's here with me because this is where she wants to be, and no one will convince me otherwise."

"What do you think, John?" asked Cart.

"Me, I've an open mind. But it certainly sounds feasible."

"I'm with the girls," Olive said, "the whole place just overflows with love."

Cart had a suggestion about the bull. "How about if I told George that dinner times I wanted to take the bull for a walk. I could take it down to my place, then back up the lane to the cows." Cart was working on a plan to train the bull to pull the trap.

"Come on," Julie said, "we have guests to attend to and a party to get ready for." She went skipping all the way.

That evening, the birthday party got under way. Julie's mum and dad were there, along with Andrew and quite a few of the villagers. A lot of the chat was about the wedding and what a special day it was going to be.

Andrew came over to share his concerns about Jenny. George and Jenny were sitting at the end of the table. George interrupted Andrew. "George marry Jenny," he said with that gorgeous smile.

"Oh, I don't think Sister will allow that," Andrew said with a smile.

"Yes," he replied. "Fred marries Julie, John marries Sarah, and George marries Jenny."

Julie went and put her arms around him. "What about if you have a special job at the wedding, and Jenny could be a bride's maid. That's very important, with a nice dress. And after the wedding we will ask Sister if Jenny can come and live with me and Fred, and you can be with her every day. It will be just like you are married.

"Do you think Sister will let her live with us?" Julie asked Andrew.

"You must think about that very carefully," he replied, "it's a lot to take on and you two are so young to burden yourselves."

"Oh, we have thought about it a lot, and it is something we want to do. Is there any legality to go through?"

"No, I wouldn't have thought so. She is over twenty-one. Legally, she can live where she likes." Andrew said he would put it to Sister.

Nearly everyone that attended the party brought a bottle, and as we know, the girls weren't used to alcohol. Two Babyshams were their limit.

As the evening progressed, the two of them where getting a little tipsy. Cart produced three bottles of homemade mead. "This is the real drink of love," he pronounced, "it's full of sweetness."

"How do you make it?" Julie asked.

"Every jar of honey my bees produce, I put my drizzle stick in and when I take it out, I let it run into an old brandy cask."

"What's a drizzle stick?" Julie said with a puzzled look.

"I have one in my pocket. It's one my father made on an old peddle lathe. I always carry it with me. It's ironic, really," he said as he pulled it from his pocket, "this is the only thing I have of my father's."

"That's a drizzle stick?" Julie said, surprised. "I thought that was a honey dipper."

"I have heard it called that before," Cart replied, "but drizzle stick sounds much better."

Julie was beginning to sound quite tipsy. She looked at Olive. "Cart has his drizzle stick," she said. "Have you got a honey pot?"

"Oh, yes, dear, I do. We use it every day. We both love are honey," she said. "Now come on, try some of Cart's mead."

Sarah and Julie both had a rather large glassful. John and Fred had been over with the guests who had attended the party. When they came back, Julie said to Fred, "Look what Cart's got; it's a drizzle stick, not a honey dipper." She was now going past being tipsy and shouldering on silly.

Fred took her to one side. "If you have any more to drink, you might blow it with Andrew. That wouldn't be fair to Jenny."

She completely sobered up in an instant and gave Fred a big kiss. "I wouldn't jeopardize that for the world," she said.

They went back and joined the others. Cart stood up. "It's time for a toast, I think," he said, banging the table with the bottom of the bottle. "I would like you all to raise your glasses and wish Fred and Julie many happy returns." Thistle and the Cornflowers started singing 'Happy Birthday'.

Andrew came and sat down amongst them. "I know

this is not the time to discuss this, but I thought as we are down in this great building I would raise it. This place is a little way out of the village, but as the village has no hall, I wondered if you would consider allowing the village to hold functions down here."

"I don't see that being a problem," John replied. "You would have to check with Fred that it didn't interfere with his guests."

The evening finished with everyone a little tipsy and singing along with Thistle and the Cornflowers.

Everyone had gone home. John and Fred had stayed down the lodge to do the final clearing up. Sarah and Julie went on up to the farm, as they thought it was time George was in bed. No matter how late it was, he still had to say good night to the owl, and the pig and the goose.

Julie and Sarah were still a little tipsy. Julie couldn't get over the word "drizzle stick'. "I can't wait to see if I can find a drizzle stick tonight," she said with a proper giggle.

"With a bit of luck, I might find one, too." Sarah was also giggling.

It wasn't long before the men were up and they were all tucked up in bed, drizzle sticks and all.

# Chapter 5

Just six weeks before the wedding, Fred and Julie were going to pick out furniture for their house. But Julie thought it would be better if she and Sarah took Jenny and sorted out her bridesmaid's dress.

John wanted to go into market, but he said he was afraid to. "You never know what I'll buy," he said, "it could be Uncle Jim, our Granny Jones, our even Aunt Fanny. Who knows?"

All the others started to laugh. Julie went over and gave him a kiss. "Dear John," she said, "you should go. Just think; you might make someone else very happy."

"You do what you think right, dear," Sarah said as they went out the door, "but I agree with Julie. The more, the merrier. Got to go and pick up Jenny."

John did go into market. First he went and looked at the cows. There was a lovely heifer, just what he was looking for. As he was looking at her, she turned, came towards him and started to lick him. "That's it, I'm not taking you home," he said to himself.

Next he went and looked at the pigs. He thought another sow would be good for the farm. This time, the pig came over and looked up and just started grunting.

"I'm losing my mind. I'm paranoid. I just don't know what to do." He was leaning on the side of the pen talking to himself.

Suddenly he felt a hand on his shoulder. "Hi, John," a voice said. It was Andrew.

"Am I glad to see you," John said, "I think I'm losing my mind." He told Andrew about the animals on the farm and what had just happened in the market.

"Does it upset you," Andrew asked, "or confuse you?"

"A bit of both, I suppose. I think I would feel better if

I knew what to believe. Can you help me with it? Do you believe these animals are who they think they are?" John asked.

"I believe we get called up in front of God when we die, then he decides quite simply, heaven or hell. But wouldn't it be reassuring if we could be returned to our loved ones when the time is right? That is what the Buddhist monks believe," Andrew said, "and who am I to argue?"

John looked at Andrew. "If it is true, how does he choose people? Why doesn't he send me my Nan? I miss her so much?"

"I can't answer that anymore than I can find a reason for so many things. You should talk to Julie, like you have me. I think she might have an answer."

"What makes you think she would have the answer," John said with the tone of disappointment. "Do you think she is a Buddhist?"

"Don't know. She is certainly someone very special, and I do wonder sometimes if God sent her to us. What a wonderful world it would be with her in charge. The only advice I can give you is this. I don't think Sarah would ever have gotten over her bereavement if she didn't believe. George seems so contented because he found his father in the bull, and as for young Jenny, who has never known happiness, she has now found her mother in a goose, as well as a new family. Surely the joy of that must do something to your heart."

"Thanks, Andrew," John said, "but I must go. I got a pig and heifer to buy."

John bought both the pig and heifer, and on his way back he called in to see Cart. When he got there, Jan Symons was there. He had a small farm up on the moors. John went up there sometimes when he was at school with one of his boys.

"Jan is selling up," Cart said. "He is going to move into Olive's cottage."

"Farming like we know it is finished. As much as I love it, we can't carry on. Mrs is just tired right out. If we try to carry on, it will kill her."

"I'm sorry to hear that. Is there anything I can do to help?" John asked.

"Well. I don't like to ask. but if you had a small bit of ground to rent, I would be grateful. You see, it's my old horse Jess. She's no good for anything, but I just don't think I could part with her," Jan said.

"There's no need to rent you a piece of ground. You can let Jess run down with the cows down by the lodge. We have taken all the gates away between the fields to let the cows and calves just roam. Jess would like it down there, and you can go down whenever you like."

"You don't know how much I appreciate that. My Mrs thinks Jess is my father come back, as he loved the place so much. She says when she turns her head, it's just like my dad did. And when she farts, she laughs, "there goes your father again"."

John looked at Cart. "Where have I heard that before?" he said with a big smile. "I must be off. The girls will be back from shopping, and I've got a pig and heifer to unload. If you need me to pick Jess up, just holler."

The girls were back from the shops and Jenny's dress was ordered. The same lady that was making the girls" was making Jenny's.

They all sat down and had tea. Fred said he would take Jenny home. George went with him. Julie had gone for a walk. John wanted to talk to her; he told Sarah all about his day. "Why don't you go and talk to her now? There are only two places she can be; either down the house or up in the meadow."

John somehow knew that she would be at the meadow. When he got there, Julie was sitting by the pond. "You look deep in thought," he said as he sat down beside her.

— *195* —

"Me, I think too much. That's my problem," she replied.

"You confuse me." John was sounding puzzled. "There is no doubt you are a lovely person. Sarah loves you to bits. I do as well, come to that."

"Hey, steady on. I'm getting married in a few weeks time," Julie replied with that beautiful smile.

"I don't mean love like that." John was embarrassed.

"Oh, that's nice, you don't fancy me, then." Julie was teasing now.

"You see what I mean, you just confuse me. I wanted a serious chat."

"You've come to the wrong person. I don't do serious."

"Perhaps that's part of your qualities; I was talking to Andrew about you today. He seems to think you can give me answers."

"Answers to what? You probably know more than I do about things."

"It's these animals that confuse me. Did you know that Christians don't believe in reincarnation? They believe in heaven and hell."

"So do I," Julie insisted, "there has to be a heaven and there has to be a hell for people like Rupert Trelivan to go to."

"So if that's the case, how do you explain the animals?"

"That's easy. How many people die in the world? Millions and millions. Now look around you. The flowers are just coming into bud, in a month this place will be full of colour that God provided, the pond – whether you come here by day with the sun shining on it or at night with the moon shining on it – it's another one of Gods bounties. Now, look over at the woods. In the summer they are a beautiful green, in the autumn they are a beautiful red and orange, and in winter there are times when they sparkle with frost. God made that. I believe God made places like this into little heavens, so that people could be in heaven with their loved ones. Just go with the flow, don't think too much about it, and I'm sure you won't be confused."

"So you are not a Buddhist, then."

"Not that I know of. Where did that come from?"

"Andrew. He said Buddhists believe in reincarnation."

"Oh, if you could take every religion in the world and mixed them all together, the real things that matter would be the same."

"What's that then?"

"Love, real love."

"Come on, are you going back now? If so, I'll walk down with you. And by the way, don't tell anyone, and I hope God won't mind, but I do fancy you. Any man would."

Julie stretched up and kissed him on the cheek. "That's nice to know."

They got back to the farm the same time as Fred and George. George went over to the barn to see the owl; he had only been gone a few moments before he was back in to fetch the others. When they got to the barn, there sitting on a ledge up under the roof were two owls, and in the corner of the ledge was the start of a nest.

"Owl got married," George said, beaming all over his face.

"We ought to leave them in peace," Fred said, "then they might have some babies."

A couple of days later, Julie and Fred returned from buying the furniture for the house. George was waiting in the yard for them. He was full of excitement. He led them to the wood shed at the side of the house, and there, tucked up between one of the rafters and the galvanize, was a nest, and the robin was sitting on it. "Robin married," he said.

That evening Andrew came around to say that he had spoken to Sister, and she would be very grateful if they could take Jenny in. "I have told her it will be after the wedding. Are you going on honeymoon?" he asked.

"Oh, I thought we might go to Tibet," Julie said. She was going to have a bit of fun with Andrew.

"Tibet?" he replied with surprise.

"Oh, yes, I thought we could go and visit the Tibetan monks. They know all about reincarnation."

"That's made things very difficult for me," Andrew replied. "You see, if you are a Buddhist, I don't know if it would be right for me to marry you."

"Oh, Andrew, I am just joking. We aren't going on a honeymoon. We have all the honey we need here in the honey pot. We even share a drizzle stick," she said with a big smile.

"Jenny can move in with us on the wedding night," she continued. "Oh, and Andrew, I do believe in heaven and hell. It's just my heavens might be a bit different from yours."

"Oh, I doubt that. I find myself warming to yours. It make a lot of sense. In fact, they have answered a lot of questions I have asked myself all my life. Now I'm off. You pair ought to come around soon and discuss the wedding; time's getting close now."

That night John had a restless one; he had things on his mind. Sarah asked what the problem was. He was reluctant to say until he was sure, in his mind, what he wanted to do. The next day he spent down at the lodge with Fred. He knew he could discuss things with him. He wanted to make sure his mind was right before he discussed it with Sarah.

They sat outside the lodge looking down the valley. George, Jenny and the visitors were in the field in front of them, with – you've guessed it – the bull, the pig and the goose. Oh, and yes, there was another member now: the latest pig John bought.

They just sat and talked for what seemed to be hours.

As it involved giving up some of what they owned, although Fred loved the idea, he could not advise one way or the other.

"You have been a great help," John said. "I must go and find Sarah and see what she has to say."

When he got up to the farm, he went into the kitchen. Sarah and Julie had just taken pasties out of the oven for the guests" lunch. "I hope there's one for me and Fred," he said as he came through the door.

Sarah stretched up and gave him a kiss. "Do you think we would leave you pair out?" she said with a smile.

"Yours are in the oven," Julie shouted as they went out the door with two large trayfuls, "and they won't be cooked until we get back."

It wasn't long before Sarah and Julie were back up and they were all sitting down to piping hot pasties. "That Aga has done well again," Fred said, ducking as he said it, as Julie raised her hand.

After lunch, John asked Sarah to go for a walk with him. They went up to Julie's Meadow, where that sat and talked. John told Sarah what he wanted to do. And if they did it, it had to be what they both wanted.

"I think that's absolutely wonderful," she said. "How we are going to go about it, and will Fred mind?"

"No, we will involve him, and I thought we could have a meeting and ask Cart and Olive over. And I don't think it would be a bad idea to involve Andrew. Oh, and there is someone else I would like to involve: Ian Symons. He and his wife are moving into Olive's cottage. Funny, really; I don't know his wife's first name. He always calls her Mrs."

Sarah put her arms around him. "I am so lucky to have you. I often look at you and Fred and think there can't be anyone in the world kinder than you pair."

"You and Julie are just the same. I think we are four lucky

individuals to have each other," John said. "Now do you want to walk a bit further?"

"No, I want you to take me up to Julie's shed and make love to me."

"What, now?"

She stood up and put her hand out to pull him up. "That's right," she said, "right now."

Back at the farm, Fred was telling Julie all about John's plans. I think she had mixed feelings; she was thinking of the future.

John and Sarah were away most of the afternoon. Julie was down at the lodge getting the tea for the guests. Sarah ran down to help her; Sarah was fidgeting about. "My, Sarah," Julie said, "if I didn't know better, I would say you got hay in your knickers."

Sarah just smiled.

"I take that as a yes, then, shall I?" Julie smiled back.

The next day Sarah went around and asked Cart and the others over for supper the following evening. When she got back, George was full of excitement, as there were four eggs in the robin's nest.

The following evening, when everyone came around, they all sat around the kitchen table. John started with a bit of a speech. "We have asked you all here as there is something Sarah and I want to do, and we would like your thoughts and input. As you know, we were left this farm, and it's probably the biggest farm in the area. We don't have to find any rent, and we don't need much money. So why do we need it all?

"So, now to my point. This week I met Jan Symons. Now, he is retiring, and he was afraid he would have to have his old faithful Jess put down. This got me thinking. There must be lots of animals whose owners don't want to have them put down, but who have come to the end of their usefulness.

"Now, this does concern Fred, because he was going to keep our cows down by the lodge, but what we want to do is put all that ground into some form of trust, so that it can always be used for animals like Jan's Jess.

"Now, what we would like is for all of you to be trustees."

Julie was the first to reply, "I think it's a lovely idea, but before you rush into it, I think you should think seriously about a few things. Firstly, this might be a big farm now, but things are changing, with tractors and combines and things. Secondly, what about when you have children? When they grow up, they might want to go into farming." She started to laugh. "It might be hard to explain to five boys that you gave their farm away. You have already been overgenerous and given us a house. Not only that, it's fine when you know the trustees, but what happens down the line, when the trustees change? Who knows what they might want to do."

"I agree with Julie," Andrew said, "haven't I always said she has wise shoulders?"

"I agree with her as well," Cart said. "Bloody nice idea though."

Fred said, "Why do you have to give the ground to a trust? I can see where Julie is coming from, and I do totally agree with her. But if you had children tomorrow, it would be fifteen or twenty years before they would start to farm. And I would hope the same trustees would be here then. So here is my suggestion; why not form a trust or committee to run it, you could lease the land for, say, fifteen years for a nominal fee of, say, a pound. Then, after that time, you would know what was right to do."

Olive said, "I would like to say that that is the most sensible thing I've heard."

"Would that be all right with you, Sarah?" asked John. "Would it still work for you and put your mind at rest?"

Andrew stood up and went around the table to where

John was sitting. "Just make sure it's what you really want," he said, putting his hand on his shoulder. "Sometimes I get the impression that you feel guilty about what you own."

"Oh, I don't feel guilty. I just think if we were blessed with all this, then surely God would want us to share it. But it's not all about land and money. That's why I want to involve all of you, because you, our dear friends, have it in abundance, and that's love for other people. So with your help, and I hope Sarah's blessing, we will lease the ground for fifteen years."

Cart stood up." If you all just hang on a minute," he said, "I'll nip home and get a bottle of mead and we can have a toast."

"No need for that," Julie said. "I kept the bottle you left at the party. But I didn't touch your drizzle stick," she said, laughing.

They all had a drink and toasted the new project. It was decided that they would run it with a committee. Cart suggested that John, Sarah, Fred and Julie should be lifetime members, so that they would always have some control of what was going on.

Andrew agreed. He also thought that they shouldn't do anything until after the wedding.

Everyone agreed.

The excitement was really building as the wedding grew ever nearer; the girls had gone for two or three dress fittings, the boys had got their suits. Cart had the bull trained to pull the trap. Four large barbeques were being assembled at the bottom of Julie's Meadow, by the pool. The plan was for the reception to be held there if it was fine; if it was wet, then they would switch to the lodge. Julie said she knew it would be dry.

John had brought the big bale trailer up for a stage for Thistle and the Cornflowers to play on. It was decide not to bring the bales of straw up for the seats until the day before.

The whole village was convinced it was going to be a day to remember.

Thistle and the Cornflowers asked if they could come up the night before and practice, as they had some modern songs they wanted to practice and they didn't know what they would be like played outside.

"That's fine," John said, "if you don't mind us being there as we are going to have a small party there instead of a stag night."

"That's fine by us. You can let us have your comments on how we perform."

Cart sent Olive into town to get some ribbon for the bull. She knew the colour of the dress. He had turned out some old horse braces he had and polished them up.

Everything was in place; the day before had arrived. Julie asked Fred if he would take her to Oakhampton to see Robert.

"Whatever for?" he replied, "You haven't mentioned him for ages."

"I know, but I still can't get it out of my mind, and I would like to understand, if it is at all possible."

"Come on, then, if that's what you want. Go and tell the others and we will go now."

They didn't talk much as they drove over the moor to Oakhampton. When they got to the farm cottages, Julie got out. "I better not look in the window this time," she said as she gave Fred a kiss.

She had been gone for over an hour. Fred was thinking about going to look for her, when suddenly they both appeared from the back of the cottages. They walked up to the car. As Fred got out, Robert came over to Fred and held his hand out "Congratulations," he said, holding his hand out for Fred to shake.

"Thank you," Fred replied.

Robert gave Julie a kiss on the cheek as they got in the car.

"Are you glad you came?" Fred asked her on the way back.

"Oh, yes, I don't think I will ever understand it. One thing that is obvious; they are both deeply in love with each other. It seems a shame that they have to keep it quiet because of what people might say."

"Do you forgive him then?"

"Oh, I forgave him ages ago." She got up as close as she could on the bench seat of the car and put her arm around him. "Let's get back and get ready for our party," she whispered. It was like a weight was lifted from her shoulders.

That night, about fifty people came to the party. Oh, yes, and a couple of pigs and a goose. John and Fred had strict orders; they had to be gone by midnight as it was unlucky to see the bride before they got to the church. John and Fred were staying at Fred's parents" place.

The flowers that seem to have been in bud for so long had suddenly burst open; the whole field was a blend of colours. If you paid someone to arrange them, you would never have got nature's arrangement.

The pond was glistening in the evening sun.

The whole evening was taken up with people chatting and drinking mead and cider; pasties and sausage rolls were in abundance, the group was playing and singing all the latest hits. After a couple of glasses of cider, Cart got up on the trailer with the band and started singing Cliff Richard hits. People had heard him singing in church, but no one could believe how good he was. He soon had everyone singing along with him.

It was now beginning to get dark. No one had noticed that Olive had slipped away. They were all too busy singing along with the music.

Then suddenly someone shouted, "Look!" Olive had been up during the day and placed candles across the middle of the meadow. She had just slipped away to light them. They spelt out "Fred and Julie, John and Sarah'. It looked absolutely beautiful; the candle lights had a slight flicker.

The evening came to an end with everyone rather merry and joyful and excited about the wedding.

Jenny was spending the night with the girls at the farm; this was the day she left the convent for good. This, of course, made George happy.

The next morning, there was so much excitement on the farm. George was up at six o'clock; he was over in the barn telling the two owls all about the day. What he didn't know was that he would be leading the bull and trap.

The hairdresser arrived at ten; the girls were running around like headless chickens. They were drunk with excitement. They didn't know what they were doing. It was a good job Olive came around and put some calm in the proceedings. "Now, sit down, dears," she said, "Let's all calm down with a cup of tea."

The time had come to get dressed. Jenny came out with her hair up, with a single carnation in one side. She had a long straight sand-coloured dress; the same as the girls" except that there was a flare at the bottom and it was cut quite low. Olive took one look at Jenny and broke out in tears, and then when the girls arrived, the tears just flowed and flowed.

Julie's mum and dad had arrived. Her dad was going in the car with her, and her mum was going to ride with Olive and Jenny. "Where is Cart?" Sarah kept asking.

"Oh, don't worry, love," Olive said, "he won't forget you."

"Oh, gosh, we have forgotten how George is getting to the church." Sarah was fretting.

"It's all arranged. Now stop worrying," Olive said. "Just concentrate on yourself."

The first car arrived, and Olive, Sarah, Julie's mum and Jenny left.

Then the second car arrived for Julie and her dad.

They were all standing outside the door. The male and female robin were sitting on the wall. It is very hard to explain, but it was like the resident robin was telling the other one all about the wedding. I'm sure the female one was telling the male that he had to look after the nest, because she was off to the wedding.

"Where is my car?" Sarah shouted. "We should be on our way. And what about George?"

With that, Cart led the bull and trap into the yard. "Are you ready, my dear," he asked.

"Is that for me?" she said, full of excitement. "Has anyone ever been to church by bull before?" Her face was a picture of joy.

"You ready, George?" Cart shouted. "You have to lead the bull."

George's face just lit up. This was the important job Fred had been telling him about.

Julie's car let Sarah and the trap go first, and then they followed on behind.

When they got to the church, they walked down the aisle together, with Cart beside Sarah, and Julie's dad beside her. They both looked extremely proud. They were followed by Olive and Jenny, with George right behind them.

Fred and John were at the altar with Andrew, waiting to conduct the service. He was looking very emotional.

Just as he was about to start the service, there was a bit of "tweet-tweet" coming from behind him. Sarah and Julie looked up and there, sitting up on the pulpit, was the robin. I'm sure she made the noise so that she was noticed.

There was hardly a dry eye in the church.

Jan Symons had taken the trap back to Cart's, and the bull back up to the cows.

When they all came out of the church, the photographer was taking photos and the robin was flying around. And suddenly the owl came and did a bit of a fly past.

It was decided that the brides and grooms would lead the guests up to the meadow.

As they approached the meadow, they could hear the group playing and singing "Here Comes the Bride'. And all the guests joined in.

The outside caterers had done a marvelous job with the barbeque.

Sarah and Julie sat down beside each other. "Do you know, it's only twelve months since me and Fred came to see you. Who would have thought so much could have happened in that short time? Do you realize we came to see you and never went home?"

"Yes," Sarah replied, "and now you're going to move into your own home. It's going to be strange without you. I do have a big secret to share with you."

"What's that?" Julie exclaimed.

"I think I'm pregnant," Sarah whispered.

Julie caught hold her hand. "Me, too," she whispered back.

"What you mean?"

"Yes, I mean, it was the night of my birthday. Cart's mead was to blame."

Sarah looked at her and smiled. "I blame that mead, as well."

"It can't take all the blame," Julie replied, "drizzle stick played his part."

They both picked up a glass of orange juice and said in tandem, "Here is to the next twelve months."